MW00763904

Swimming Naked With My Dog –

The Secrets Between Us

By Amy Rowen
with assistance, as always,
from Julie Rowen

ISBN: 978-1-932984-64-1

Printed in the United States

This book is dedicated to Julie Rowen...

...an extraordinary dog that left a trail of extraordinary memories.

Julie had many roles in life; a service dog, agility champion, flyball and dock diving competitor, dancer and amateur tracker. She was known and appreciated by many but her accomplishments only depict things she did, not who she was. My hope is that this novel will allow others to have a window into her heart. Julie had a lot of heart.

I am grateful for the dedicated, professional, and understanding service that **Dr. James Eldridge and Dr. Caryn Scaravelli** at Chagrin Animal Clinic have provided for more than 25 years. Their support and advocacy was especially valuable when we were confronted with critical medical issues where decisions and management of care made the difference between life, quality of life, or death.

Dr. Ellen Belknap, at Metropolitan Veterinary Hospital in Ohio, is commended for going above and beyond the usual standard of care by researching and aquiring canine contact lenses (from Germany) so that Julie's quality of life was not compromised by her aging eyesight.

Thank you to the Oncology Department at Ohio State Veterinary Hospital, especially **Dr. Joelle Fenger and Joelle Nielson, MSW.** Although I am appreciative for the patience and kindness that you showed me, I am mostly grateful for the loving attention that Julie recieved from you during those few, but tormenting, hours when we had to be separated by walls while she recieved treatment.

I would be remiss not to mention Julie's extended family, **Jill Quirk, Becca Quirk and Katie Loucks, Daisy and Bogey.** No matter where the paths in life take us in the future, we walked a lovely, adventurous and enlightning path together that we will always share in our hearts. You made Julie's life richer. Thank you.

I am lucky that my close friend, **Julie (Zurfluh) Rosenberger,** lied to me about how easy-going yellow labradors are. Had I known the truth there is a chance that I would have missed out on a profound and spiritual relationship.

Lastly, I must extend special gratitude to **Greta Marchus** who provided invaluable relationship counseling to me and Julie that aided me in developing a deeper understanding and empathy of canine behaviour. At times you were Julie's voice and you enabled us to communicate on a profound level. As a result Julie was empowered to teach me a great deal as well.

In April 2012 the Julie Rowen Foundation was established to provide resources and hospice care for canines with cancer, with a special emphasis on service dogs. Too many service dogs provide invaluable and selfless service to grateful humans that lack the proper resources to reciprocate when faced with the dogs' end of life care. More information can be found at **www.JulieRowenFoundation.org.**

Chapter 1

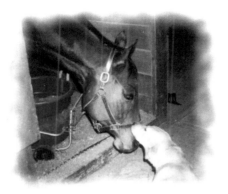

I should have called first. I realize that now. Several years ago I drove down a long gravel drive bordered by large trees. The first thing I noticed was that the trees have faces. Hmmm.

As I reached what is probably the midway point in the drive I started to notice various signs. "Dogs Welcome, People Tolerated," read the first sign. The next sign was faded but I could still make out an image of a caricature of a yellow dog chasing a duck, or was it a ball? The sign read "Yellow Lab at Play." The third sign, and by far my favorite, was a large Caution sign that warned "CAUTION: Young Dogs, Old Dogs, and One Stupid Dog at Play." Throughout the time I knew the dogs my opinion of which one was the "stupid" dog changed from day to day. Well, with the exception of Julie. There was never a day when I looked into Julie's eyes and saw stupid.

I passed what I recognized to be a barn on the left, and drove to the driveway that led to the house. There was a third, smaller, building but I was unable to discern what it was. Until I read the sign, "Doggie Athletic Center," which was slightly hidden by a solar light. Still chuckling to myself about the second to last sign that I had read, I started to get out of my truck and the door to the smaller building flew open. Several dogs ran outside, wet and happy. "Must have been bath day," I figured. All the dogs were black except one. There was one blonde puppy. An unaware woman trudged through the doorway with a cigarette in one hand, a towel over her head and wearing what I would call barn boots....otherwise, she was naked. Yes, *naked*. She started to call after her dogs when she spotted me. We both froze for a beat then she grabbed the towel from her hair and put it around her short, slightly chubby frame.

The optimism that I had felt in my gut diminished. I probably was not going to be the new Farrier. I had spoken to the woman several weeks ago when her former Farrier, as she put it, "was no longer with them."

I pretended to watch the dogs as they rolled and rubbed themselves on the dry grassy lawn. One by one they stood up and shook off the excess water. I had to give up the pretense when the woman barked "Can I help you?" There was an irritated edge in her voice. Nope, I thought, not going to get the job. "Uh, I shoulda called first," I stammered.

I thought it was best not to walk toward her with my hand held out for a handshake. "Sorry to bother you. We spoke on the phone several weeks ago. I'm Ron, the Farrier. Are you Amy?"

"Yep," she sighed. "Well, I obviously wasn't expecting you today. I was swimming with my dogs in their pool in the dog gym."

I was not sure how to respond to that. Truth be told I wanted to jump back into my truck and retreat. Problem was I was too afraid of running over one of the dogs so I stood there looking befuddled. "Well, Ma'am, you said you wanted to meet me and see me with the horses before you made a decision about a new Farrier. I was

6

in the area….." my voice trailed off. "I actually did try to call but I got a voice mail message."

"Well that should've been your first clue that I was otherwise indisposed." Another sigh, "Well okay. By the way don't call me Ma'am."

By now the dogs were running all around me and one kept jumping up and trying to grab my arm.

"Debbie, off!" the woman scolded. She reached for the dog's collar and the towel dropped. "Crap," she said as she gathered the towel up.

Definitely, definitely not getting the job. How to bow out gracefully? I wondered.

"I can come back at a better time." I turned to leave.

She held up her hand and said, "Stay." When I frowned she added, "Well just wait here. I'll be right back" and then she turned toward the lawn and called out, "Girls!" Every single dog stopped and stared at her as if hanging on her next word.

"House!" There it was but it must not have been the word they had hoped for because they all looked disappointed as they trotted toward the door. When I heard the door slam behind Amy I knew I had my chance to escape. I took too long in the debate because within just a few minutes she emerged from the house wearing shorts and a long t-shirt, and the boots. She was still wearing the boots. The blonde puppy from the group trotted alongside of her. The puppy leapt in circles in front of me while her owner paused to light another cigarette. I got the sense that the awkward silence amused her in some way, as if she were toying with me. I cleared my throat.

Silence. Amy walked briskly by me, her puppy at her side trying to chew on her boots as she moved toward the barn. When I didn't move she paused and called over her shoulder, "Come on…." The puppy, too, glanced back at me with a curious look.

I reluctantly followed the two to the barn. Shrugging off my initial embarrassment I rubbed my forehead with the back of my hand as I entered. The yellow puppy ran past Amy into the hay area. She jumped playfully on the bales of hay. Amy looked pained. "No! Julie!"

The puppy looked up and wagged her tail. Her tongue hung out of her grinning mouth.

I could tell Amy was trying to suppress a smile. She walked over to the hay room and plucked the puppy from her jungle gym. She returned to me carrying a wriggling Julie under her arm.

"What?" she asked when she looked my way?

I shrugged at her. "Nothin'. Well, she sure is a cute puppy!"

"She's a pain in the ass. But she is a puppy so I keep her with me at all times," Amy stated. The pup was still dangling under the woman's arm. "I've never had a puppy this bad. I have had dogs all of my life, but never this bad." She held the puppy up and in front of her face. "I wish I knew what was going through her mind." Nose to nose Amy asked Julie, "Will you tell me all of your secrets? Huh? Will you?"

"Awful little, though. I've never seen a puppy that little."

"She is only four weeks old," Amy explained as she lowered the puppy. "She should still be nursing from her mother, but some asshole dropped her and her four brothers in a dumpster. Box was duct taped up and everything." She was talking tough but I could see tears well in her eyes. Julie resumed tugging on her owners

8

boots. Amy glanced down at the small pup and grumbled, "pain in the ass."

I slowly walked forward. My feet sunk into something plush. I looked down, "I, I, I've never been in a barn that was carpeted." I glanced up. "Or with a flat screen TV for the horses." Once inside the front doors the short hallway intersected with an aisle way that ran about 1200 feet. There were other rooms off the aisle way such as the hay room, a wash stall, and a tack room. All of the horses were housed on the right leg of the aisle, three on the right and two on the left. The TV was positioned so they could all see it. I couldn't help but notice that there were cameras in the ceilings as well.

There was a sudden engine noise and vapor started to pour from the ceiling. I jumped back in an effort to avoid getting wet. "What is that?" The puppy, Julie, glanced up at her owner and I do believe she rolled her eyes.

Amy smiled at the pup and explained. "It's a misting system. It keeps the dust down and we've added aromatherapy to the water. In the summer months we include fly spray," she explained as she gently placed Julie on the carpet. Julie immediately started digging at the carpet and tugging on loose threads with her puppy teeth.

"All barns have flies. It's unavoidable." I stated.

"Find one," Amy challenged as she pulled Julie into her arms again.

I rubbed my forehead with the back of my hand and glanced around the barn. "Hmph. I'll be…"

For the first time Amy grinned. Feeling more at ease, I pushed on with the business at hand. "When were your horses feet trimmed last?" I asked, leaning over the door of a horses stall. The horse leapt straight up in the air and shuffled to the back of his stall. He leaned against the wall and snorted nervously.

I felt a tug at the back of my shirt so I stepped backwards several feet. Amy shook her head sadly. "That is Milton. He has some serious psychological problems. You'll need to earn his trust. He is actually very gentle, just scared of everything."

"Have you tried drugs?" I asked as I reached over to pat the top of the puppy's head.

"For me or my horse?" she quipped.

"Uh. I was thinking the horse, but..." I decided against completing my thought.

With crossed arms Amy swung toward me as the puppy simultaneously ducked from my reach. "I do not drug my horses. My relationship with them is based on trust and respect." She snarled as she pulled the pup into her arms then reached for Milton's stall door.

I was more comfortable out of the way since it was apparent that Amy was going to bring the whack-job out of his stall. The door slowly swung wide and Amy turned and walked away. She pivoted toward the horse and made a hand signal with the hand that was not clutching the puppy. Milton tentatively approached the open door. He dropped his head and sniffed the ground before placing his left foot onto the carpet, as if to test the stability of the surface. He slowly made his way out of his stall, gave me a suspicious glance and walked to Amy. She put her hand up and he halted. She turned and walked toward an indoor arena and the horse walked beside her. Inside the arena I watched in awe as the two of them seemed to dance. When she stopped, so did he. When she resumed walking, so did he. When she walked briskly, so did he. When she stopped abruptly, so did he. The horse followed his owners lead without a halter or lead line. His head remained by her shoulder at all times. I moved aside as the two passed me and Amy guided Milton into his stall. Once again in his stall Amy commanded, "Turn," and the horse swung around to face her. She gently stroked his face and he nuzzled her neck. Julie stretched her neck and gave the horse a gentle sniff. They all seemed to be in the moment except that, over Amy's shoulder, the horse glared at me. I was uncertain how I was to earn his trust. Amy backed up and faced me. Amy scratched Julie behind her ears while she spoke to me. "All of my horses are rescues so they all have problems of one kind or another. That is why I want to see how they respond to you before you try to work on their feet. For their safety and yours…"

The introductions continued and we all seemed to develop a friendly rapport. There were four horses and a spirited Pony. The last horse that I met was Hammlet. As Hammlet pawed at the floor of his stall and inquisitively turned his head, Amy smiled. "He is my f-a-v-o-r-i-t-e."

I stretched to pat Hammlet. "Aw. You shouldn't have a favorite."

Amy grimaced as Julie happily spun in circles, wagging her tail. "She knows that word."

I made a face "I would think so. It's obvious that SHE is the favorite of all of the dogs."

With a frown she stated, "First, she knows that word because she has a FAVORITE treat. Secondly, I would die, or kill, for any of my girls. But Julie is a puppy. I keep her with me at all times, until she grows older of course."

I was skeptical. I didn't have much of a chance to observe this woman with her other dogs but it seemed to me that there was an unspoken bond between her and her puppy.

As I walked back I passed Milton again, and he ran to the back of his stall, only stopping because there was a wall. Amy and Julie exchanged glances. Frankly, the pup was adorable but she was actually starting to creep me out because she seemed to understand some unspoken communication between her and her owner.

A young man strutted into the barn while I was contemplating the puppy. He pulled his sunglasses off as he entered, using the back of his wrist to push his cowboy hat back further on his head.

He ignored me and said to Amy, "Hey. Did ya see the paper?"

She shook her head. "Why?"

He chortled, "Oh. You're gonna looooove this. Hold on, I'll go grab my copy."

Amy returned to explaining the horse's different quirks. Most had physical limitations, all but Milton.

The young man returned to the barn clutching a newspaper. He repeated his previous routine with the sunglasses and the hat, and then held the paper, open to a folded page, to Amy.

As Amy bowed her head to search the page, he pointed at a paragraph in the classifieds.

Amy looked up and stared at the young man. "Greg, what IS this?"

"What it says."

Amy, shaking her head read distinctly, "Anyone who has worked for Amy Rowen please contact me to organize revenge."

I raised my eyebrows. Boy! This lady knows how to piss people off!

"Call it."

Greg looked confused. "What? Why?"

"So I know what he is planning. I mean, I can hold my own but I want to be sure he isn't planning on hurting the horses in some way. Or burning the house down with the dogs inside. I also plan on calling the police. If he hurts any of the animals, I will personally kill him myself." She said the last sentence in a calm manner, which frankly, was more alarming to me.

Greg looked at me with wide eyes and nodded vigorously. "She'll do it too! She killed a guy that hit her horse with a pitch fork five years ago. She said she'd kill him and one morning, he was gone. His stuff was at his apartment on the farm, but he was gone. Never saw him again."

Amy stared at Greg until he finished his story. "Greg?"

He swung his head toward her.

"Get to work. We'll call this guy together later."

Greg pivoted and strutted toward the closest outside paddock where I saw him dump a large water tub and begin scrubbing it.

I looked at Amy out of the corner of my eye. She laughed. "I didn't kill the guy. Truth is I am curious why he left. I must have really scared him. He hit my horse with a pitchfork badly. She needed 16 stitches. My first priority was obviously to get her stitched her up, then out of that boarding facility. Late that day, after I got April on the trailer I walked back into the barn office and popped my head through a crack in the door. I told him I'd be back later to deal with him, but not right away. He won't be expecting me and that'll be my advantage. "

Amy glanced again at the paper. "What an idiot." She sighed and shook her head. "Idiots can be dangerous, though. Now I am even happier that I fired him."

"What did he do?" I asked

"What do you mean?"

"To get fired."

"Oh. He didn't show up for work for two weeks. Well, after the first day we considered him gone. He shows up two weeks later and insists he was on a mission for the FBI and his absence couldn't be helped. He demanded he get paid for the last two weeks as well. It doesn't take much to get fired here. As soon as someone shows poor character they are out of here. It's like hiring a responsible babysitter, except my babies happen to be animals."

We turned back toward the horses. Standing shoulder to shoulder I asked, "Who is April?"

Amy ignored me.

I turned my head toward her and looked at her face. She had grimaced but she continued to ignore me.

I then spent another hour harnessing and leading the horses around the barn. At one point I requested a piece of paper and a pen because I felt the need to take notes. I was due to return in four weeks to trim feet and replace the shoes. While I was jotting down notes Greg passed by me. "Okay ta let'em out now?" He asked Amy.

"Are all the pasture gates shut?" she queried.

"Yup!" He stated with confidence and pride.

I said my good-byes and reassured Amy I'd be back in four weeks. I felt a tugging on my boots and glanced down. The puppy tried to attack my bootlaces. Amy picked her up and apologized.

I caught myself holding my breath as I drove down the long gravel drive. When I was halfway down the driveway three thoroughbreds sped past me and crossed the street. In my rearview mirror I could see Greg hauling ass after them. I chuckled to myself. He is SO fired, I thought. I didn't think he would join allegiance with the guy that had the ad in the paper. Greg really seemed to believe Amy had, and would, kill somebody. My mind was quiet for a beat then I nodded as I thought, I could see that.

* * *

Chapter 2

It was fall and the coloured leaves gently fell on the hood of my truck as turned into the driveway of the barn. I was early because I skipped lunch. For reasons I cannot explain I felt anxious about getting back to the small farm in Geneva. Accustomed to large boarding facilities where horses are boarded and often forgotten I looked forward to the intimate relationship the horses had with their owner in Geneva.

I slammed the door to my truck and stared at the sky for a moment as I stretched. So much of my job entails driving from farm to farm. Sauntering into the barn I noticed a soft classical music playing. I was trying to identify how I knew the piece when the yellow puppy startled me. She popped her head from the tack room and eyed me inquisitively. I could tell she was itching to follow me as I walked down the aisle to the arena. She didn't, but she wanted to. I leaned against the door to the arena and watched Amy as she laid flat across a horses' back. As the horse trotted she slowly rose from the waist, swung her legs back and then stood on the horses back. It was then that I realized she was not holding reins, probably because the horse was not wearing a bridle. As she stood she slowly started to turn. Then she spotted me in the doorway and her body language went from relaxed to rigid. She fell. Although the fall was soundless the yellow dog, Julie as I remember, bolted by me to Amy's side. Clearly the dog's instincts were better than mine were, because I stood frozen. The horse trotted to a corner and stood, looking worried. Julie started to lick Amy's face and drew laughter from the tough woman. As she rolled on her side to pull herself to her feet the laughter stopped abruptly as she locked eyes with me. "You're early," she snapped.

I shuffled backwards to make room for her to exit and she brushed passed me, Julie at her side. "Sorry." I mumbled. I followed her into the barn. "Want me to get your horse?" I asked.

Amy whistled and all at once Julie jumped behind her and the horse sauntered into the barn. He looked at Amy for direction and she pointed. "Stall," she said. I could swear the horse nodded as he walked into the stall that said "Hammlet" above it.

"Start with Milton," she said. I paused to read the names on the stalls. Julie cocked her head and stared at me. I swear she was thinking that I am an idiot for not remembering who everyone is. Her attention quickly switched to her owner. "Arooooh, arooooh," she howled. Amy glanced at her and nodded. Julie trotted over to Amy's side and pawed at her. "I'll be back," she stated. "Go ahead and put Milton in the cross ties." She briskly walked toward her house, Julie trotting alongside.

I shrugged and entered Milton's stall with his halter dangling from my left hand. He swung his backside around toward me. I gently placed my right hand on his rump and stroked him as I walked toward his head. He turned his head away for a moment then turned toward me and snorted. I stroked his long face and gently placed the halter on his head. I led him out of his stall and slowly down the aisle. I allowed him to stand in front of the wash stall for a while before luring him into it. I reached in my pocket and pulled out a few pieces of carrot. As he was crunching on the carrot Amy and Julie returned. Julie's expression showed disappointment as she noticed the horse. She hung her head and walked into the tack room where she stayed, peering out of the open door.

"Sorry. I had to take some medication," Amy apologized.

Hmm. Medication? I thought. Well that does make sense. If anyone could benefit from pharmaceuticals it would be this woman, or anyone around her.

One by one I trimmed the horses' feet and replaced their shoes. Amy didn't speak to me at all over the three hours, other than to explain the horses' different anxieties. "Lucy was hit by the last Farrier with a hammer. She has some serious trust issues." Amy stood before the horse and spoke softly while I worked on Lucy's hind feet. I was preoccupied with wondering what happened to the last Farrier. After all she did say he was no longer with us....

The horses were all good horses. They may have all been rescues with one problem or another but they were well behaved, polite, well tempered. As soon as the pony was put back in his stall Julie exited the tack room and returned to Amy's side. I don't think the puppy ever took her eyes off her owner in the entire three hours.

"She really adores you. What's your secret?"

Amy smiled at Julie, "We'll never tell."

As I packed up my truck a man on a tractor drove by. I waved and he nodded back. Husband? Boyfriend? Worker?

Amy walked by me and handed me a check. She noticed me staring at the man on the tractor. "That's my brother," she answered as if reading my mind. "He owns the farm, too."

I thanked her for the check and pulled a receipt from my book and handed it to her. "Usually I try to keep the horses on a six week schedule. Will that be okay?"

"Sure, but they may start pulling shoes around five weeks in the summer," she explained.

"I'll put them down for five weeks then if that is better," I offered. She nodded and walked toward the house with Julie tagging along as usual. Amy looked down at her puppy and smiled wide. When she looked at this puppy, I realized, was the only time I ever saw her smile. She softened around the horses but only smiled at the puppy.

* * *

Chapter 3

W inter was uneventful, other than the two occasions when I got my truck in the barn drive in Geneva. I cannot even say that I got to know Amy better over the course of this time. She didn't chat with me much and often her replies to my comments or questions were sarcastic. Her attention was usually monopolized by the horses while she held them for me to work on their feet.

Finally, Spring had sprung and I returned to the farm. As I pulled down the driveway five dogs ran toward my truck. They seemed to be all ages. One of them tripped over her own feet and I wondered if she was the dog referred to in one of the signs: "Drive Slowly, old dogs, young dogs, and one stupid dog at play." Really, none of them looked stupid. They were all black. One dog stopped about ten feet away from me and barked. She was wagging her tail as she barked, sending me mixed messages, much like her owner. I glanced around the open yard and finally spotted the blond puppy in the water. She was swimming in circles. Then I spotted a woman's head bobbing in the water, Julie circling. There was a sharp whistle and the dogs all ran back toward the dock where they had been playing before I interrupted them. Julie climbed from the pond and shook the water off of her coat. This was unnecessary because she spun around and took a running leap off of a long dock, landing inches from her owner. I stopped the truck in the drive and hopped out. I walked toward the dock and was soon surrounded again by black dogs, wagging their tails and greeting me gleefully. Perhaps Amy had forgotten our appointment. As I walked closer to the dock I noticed Amy swimming further away, Julie by her side. She waved. I waved back. I drew closer so I could hear what she was yelling through her laughter. Hmm. Go figure, the woman laughs.

I heard another call but from another direction. I turned and spotted a young woman waving at me. "I'm going to hold the horses for you today. Come on to the barn, please."

I stared out into the pond at Amy and Julie who had been joined by two of the other dogs.

I shrugged and turned back toward my truck, just one dog at my heels.

The other woman bellowed, "Debbie, come." The dog named Debbie ran toward the young woman as I pulled myself into my truck. I slowly drove down the driveway to the barn, taking frequent glances at Amy and the dogs swimming. "Isn't that something?" I said to myself.

First Amy seemed almost overly concerned about the handling of her horses. Now it seems as if she could not be bothered to oversee them. As I slid out of my truck I could hear happy barking and even uncharacteristic giggling from Amy. Debbie raced past me toward the noise of fun as I stepped into the barn. One of the horses was wandering loose around the barn. He had the short mane, no white markings. I remembered him as Hammlet. He walked over to me and as I reached out to pat him he grabbed the back of my shirt and playfully tugged. "Hey!" I exclaimed with a grin. I heard laughter as the tack room door slid open. "Hammy, stop it!" the young woman commanded. The horse proudly trotted in circles in his stall before having a sip of water from his water bucket. I walked over to shut his stall door and the horse nodded his head vigorously at me and grinned. What a clown, I thought.

"Hammlet is just a big goof, he was just having fun." The woman reached out and patted Hammlet on his head. "By the way, I'm Kris."

"I am supposed to do the horse's feet today. Did Amy forget?"

Kris shook her head. "No. She asked me to come in early and help."

"Okay. I guess she must not think much of me. I tried to talk to her outside but she actually swam away. Did I offend her?" I asked, but I was thinking to myself that she was just a bitch.

"I don't think so." Kris answered. "She was probably naked."

Before I could process Kris' reply she continued, "She doesn't like to be in the barn much unless she is working with the horses. Her first horse, April, died last winter." She nodded toward the first stall that sat empty except for many cards nailed on the wall and a spray of fresh flowers in the hay rack.

I walked over to the stall and looked at the wall. How did I not notice this before? I spotted a large portrait with an obituary and I recognized it from the local paper. I turned toward Kris, "I remember seeing that in the paper right after New Year's Day. It was a full page. I didn't know that was her horse, of course, I didn't know her then."

"You still don't know her." Kris said. There was a snap to her words but she smiled at me as she said them.

"She keeps fresh flowers in the hay rack," I mumbled mostly to myself as I walked by the stall again with Hammlet, heading to the wash stall.

Kris was considerably more talkative than her employer. We chatted about everything from the hunter jumper circuit to our favorite TV commercials. While she was slowly feeding pieces of carrot to Lucy, another, but different young man entered the barn. He made a beeline for Kris. "Can you believe this?" he quickly continued, not waiting for a reply. "My dog is sick so I take her to the vet, right?" Another rhetorical question. "So the vet says she is pregnant! I go, no way. We only have two dogs. A Jack Russell Terrier and her, a lab. So, uh, the vet goes, is your other dog a male? I say, well yeah. She goes, is he fixed? I say no. So she said then my lab is probably pregnant because she isn't fixed either, right? I say no way. One is a Jack Russell and she is a Lab. They are different kinda dogs so they wouldn't be attracted to each other." He ends his story emphatically indignant. Kris and I exchanged worried glances. As the new guy marched to the tack room to punch in for the day Kris muttered, "I don't see him lasting long, do you?"

I grinned. "Uh. No."

"You wanna make it interesting?" She smiles

"What do you mean?" I asked

"Bet on how many days he lasts." Kris is still smiling.

"I am guessing that there is a high turnover rate here?" I smiled.

"You could say that." Kris admitted. "Bet?"

"Okay. Sure. What are the stakes?"

She looked thoughtful. "How about 50 bucks?"

"This isn't really fair. You know Amy better so you know what she will and will not put up with. I only met her that once and…."

Kris interrupted. "You may have only met her once but are you really trying to tell me you have no idea how protective she is with her animals?"

I nodded, an image of Amy beating a farm hand to death with a pitchfork. "Okay. 50 it is. I say a week."

Kris' smile grew. "It's a bet. I say two days."

I raised my eyebrows and held out my hand past Lucy. Lucy nuzzled my hand, hopeful it contained a carrot. Kris and I both smiled and we shook on our bet.

Kris was returning Lucy to her stall and I began sweeping. As I was sweeping the floor of the wash stall Julie pranced into the barn, followed by Amy. Julie wagged her tail at me and shook water off her coat. I jumped back, "Why do dogs always do that?" I asked.

"What? Shake?" Amy asked.

"No. I know why they shake but why do they have to be right next to ME when they do it?"

Amy didn't answer but she did smile a little….or was she showing her teeth? She pulled a check from her checkbook and handed it to me.

"Looked like you were having fun out there." I attempted benign conversation.

She nodded. "Yep, I love swimming with my dogs, they can't tell when I'm crying when I'm in the water." She pivoted and walked away. As Julie turned to follow she glanced at me over her shoulder.

I resumed sweeping up my mess. I stopped and lifted my head to take a whiff of the air. When Kris got closer I said to her, "You smell smoke?"

Kris sniffed the air and her eyes got wide as smoke starting pouring from underneath the tack room door. As she lunged for the door handle I stopped her. "Wait. The fire is contained. Get the horses out first. Fires can really erupt when they get more oxygen."

Kris ran down the barn aisle swinging stall doors open. She then turned back and started encouraging the horses to move toward one of the pasture doors. I was hanging up my cell phone when she closed a gate behind them. "What are you doing?" she snapped. "Taking pictures or texting your girlfriend?"

Ooh. Snippy, I thought. I replaced my phone in my back pocket. "I called the fire department."

Not surprisingly the view of fire trucks turning down her drive-way had Amy racing to the barn. Julie was at her heels. "What happened?" she demanded as she entered the smoke filled corridor.

"I don't know. Jerry came in to clock in then he left. I think he went to the back pasture to mend fences."

I glanced out the door. "I still see a truck in the driveway. A red one. Does it belong to either of you?"

Both women shook their heads as they stood back to allow two firemen to pass them with a long hose.

"You guys are fast." Kris observed.

"Everybody out of the barn. This thing could explode when we open it," a fireman growled.

We all turned toward the exit and ran out of the barn. Amy looked down. "Where is Julie?" She panicked.

We looked all over the yard. Amy swung around and sped back into the barn. She was only gone about a minute when Jerry joined Kris and me. He stood between us and gazed at the barn, smoke pouring out of the whole building. His face showed awe. "Woooowww. Cooool," he stammered.

I leaned back so I could make eye contact with Kris. She caught my gaze and shrugged. "Rats. I should have bet on one day."

Our attention was brought back to the barn when a small explosion erupted. Kris took a big step toward the barn and stopped. "Oh my God! Amy and Julie…." Her speech trailed off.

"Glad to know you care." Amy's voice was behind us. Kris moved to embrace Amy, holding Julie. Amy raised her hand and said, "Fight the urge."

"Where were you?" I asked.

"Julie isn't an idiot. She had run through the arena into the side pasture. She was huddled behind the water tub."

Once again Jerry, still distracted by the scene, muttered. "This is so cool." Kris and I looked toward Amy. As Amy started to open her mouth Kris and I joined in. "You're fired."

Jerry laughed. "Fired, ha! Get it? Fired?"

The rest of us stood and stared at Jerry as he slowly sauntered to his truck, hands in his pockets and murmuring "Soo Cooool."

* * *

Chapter 4

"Milton lost a shoe at 1926 Barnum," the message stated. I shook my head as I pressed the replay button. "Milton lost a shoe at 1926 Barnum," the message repeated. I sighed and looked at my schedule for the next day. I had clients scheduled that were two hours away. Aware that Amy preferred to have someone in the barn when I was shoeing horses I dare not show up late tonight while she is asleep, although it was tempting. It was only 10 o'clock at night. I took a chance and phoned Amy.

"Hello?" Amy answered.

I explained my situation. "I apologize if I'm calling too late. I will be in Akron most of the day tomorrow. I could get out to your barn tonight, in about an hour, or very early tomorrow."

"Whatever you prefer. Just let me know in advance," she replied.

"How 'bout I head over now?"

"Sure. See you in an hour." She hung up. I could not be sure if she was irritated or not. Truthfully, I didn't care much because the world does not revolve around her.

I caught myself fuming about how cold and selfish Amy was. Why did I even take this job? There are plenty of Farriers. She claims she is picky about the kind of care her horses have but it isn't as if I'm the best Farrier in the area. Okay, I am the best. That only explains why she wanted me as a Farrier. It doesn't explain why I had to agree to the job. What is wrong with me? I became irritated with myself so I punched the CD button and played "Big'n'Rich" loud. My temper cooled as I drew closer to Barnum Road. When I stepped from my truck to open the driveway gate I could see the glow of eyes sparkle ten feet away. It was then that I heard the footsteps on the gravel and then a soft voice.

"I was going to open the gate for you," Amy said as she reached to pull the gate open.

"Oh. Thanks." I wasn't sure what to say. "Want a ride back to the barn?"

She hesitated then nodded. She opened the passenger side door of my truck then slapped her leg and said "up." Julie leapt gracefully into my truck. The puppy was growing up fast. With Julie between us we rode in uncomfortable silence to the barn. As Amy slid from the truck I thought I heard her say "Thanks."

I gathered my gear and followed Amy and Julie into the barn. After sliding the tack room door open so that Julie could take cover, she opened Milton's stall door and made a kissing sound. The horse didn't move. Amy frowned and patted the side of her leg. "Move out," she said. Milton dropped his head and snorted. "This isn't like him," she muttered as she grabbed his halter from the front of the stall door. She walked into the stall, put the halter on the horse's head and pulled him forward from his stall. Milton limped terribly. Amy halted the horse. "He was not doing that before," she said with concern in her voice.

I groaned. "This doesn't look good. A missing shoe shouldn't cause three legged lameness. Don't move him any further."

"Duh." Amy said as she looked up from the horse's foot to me. We both laughed. I don't know why, perhaps it was stress.

"I'll stand with him. You call the vet." I offered as I reached for Milton's lead line.

Amy silently complied and walked into the tack room for the phone. I could hear her calmly explaining the situation to someone until her voice was overcome by Julie's whining. I saw Amy hold her hand over her free ear and turn away from her dog. When she hung up the phone she praised Julie. When Amy exited the tack room Julie stood in the doorway restlessly.

I nodded toward the dog, "What's wrong with her?"

Amy glanced over her shoulder at Julie. "Nothing. She was alerting me to the fact that my heart rate skyrocketed."

I was skeptical. "How can she tell?"

"Apparently my body odor changes. She alerts to complicated migraines, high heart rates, high blood pressure, seizures and intoxication."

"That's a shame because I really could use a beer," I snorted.

Amy glared at me. I shrugged it off. "I was just kidding. How do you know what Julie is trying to tell you?" Changing the subject but still skeptical.

"The type of alert."

"Hmm. Okay, if you say so."

Amy glared at me. "She's kept me alive so far. She has never been wrong either, my dog doesn't lie."

"But she is just a puppy," I said

Amy shrugged. "I know. I didn't even know dogs, or ah... puppies could do such a thing. It took me forever to put her weird noises and my health issues together." As if catching herself sharing personal information she abruptly turned her back to me, walked over to Milton and took his lead from me. "You can go. I'm sorry you drove all the way out here. You obviously won't be able to do anything with him tonight. Let me get him back in his stall and I'll grab my wallet." I watched as she gently backed Milton back into his stall.

"You don't owe me anything, but I'd like to stay and see what the vet says."

She shrugged. "I can call you. I have to owe you something for the drive out and your time."

I slowly shook my head and raised my hand. "It's no problem. Really."

She stormed into the tack room and returned with a check, shoving it in my direction. "I don't like to owe anyone anything."

"I'd rather stay. You never know, maybe they will need me. I'm not keen on vets playing Farrier in my absence. Besides I'm worried about my horse."

Amy frowned, "Your horse?"

"Well, you know, my client, horses, uh, client." I shrank from her glare.

Amy slid down the wall to the sitting position. Julie curled up with her, with her head laid gently in her owner's lap. Amy looked down at her sleeping dog and whispered something. Julie's tail thumped on the floor but she didn't open her eyes.

"What did you say?" I asked.

Amy raised her head at me and frowned. "It's private."

"It isn't polite to tell secrets in front of others," I argued.

Amy ignored me and continued whispering to her pup, eye-balling me as she did so. Julie's tail continued to thump as she, too, stared at me.

To avoid further awkwardness I walked out to my truck and pulled a pack of cigarettes from the top of my dashboard. I leaned against the truck and stared at the stars. A thin layer of clouds passed above me. I was startled by the sudden approach of Amy. She reached out, took my cigarette from my grip and took a long drag before returning it.

Without a word she and Julie passed by me and I watched as they walked toward the house. I saw a glow of light as the front door opened and several dogs burst through the threshold. The dogs ran around the yard and jumped at each other, barking happily. Julie joined in the mêlée. This was the first time I witnessed Julie behaving like a normal dog. Amy slowly approached a child's elaborate swing set and took a seat on a swing. My thoughts wandered to wondering who the swing set belonged to. Did Amy have children? Perhaps the swing set was already on the property when she and her brother purchased the farm.

My thoughts were interrupted by the glow of headlights at the end of the long drive. Amy spotted them too because she stood up and called her dogs back to the house. Once all the dogs, all but Julie, were secured in the house, Amy returned to the barn just ahead of the vehicle. I watched as the vet's truck backed down the barn drive and parked just in front of my truck.

I gaped at the young woman who slid from the truck. She was not your stereotypical vet. This woman had long flowing blond hair that she brushed over her shoulder as she grabbed a large medical bag from the back seat. As she approached the barn I could see a sparkle in her blue eyes. She smiled at me as she passed. She reminded me of the head cheerleader at my high school. I crushed my third cigarette out under my boot and followed the vet into the barn. Amy looked over as I entered. "Ron, this is Emily. Emily, Ron," she said as she waved casually in my direction. I nodded at Emily as she marched into Milton's stall. Amy and I both leaned over the stall and watched Emily palpate the horse's leg. Julie watched from just inside the tack room. Emily glanced over at the obedient young dog and said, "She is SO well behaved. What is your secret?"

Amy smiled a Mona Lisa smile and shrugged. Then she returned our attention to Milton.

Milton pulled his leg from Emily's grasp. She sighed. "Well, let's get him into the wash stall and get some x-rays." I looked toward Amy and caught her staring at the stall next door, April's. She nodded at Emily's instruction as she pulled the lead line from the hook on the horse stall. With authoritative motion Amy pulled Milton from his stall and led him, limping, into the wash stall. Milton snorted and sputtered as I helped attached the cross ties to his halter. Emily was busy pulling items from the back of her truck.

After x-rays had been taken we all crowded around a small computer screen. Emily groaned as she pointed to an area of the screen. "See that? That is a stress line fracture."

I glanced over Emily's head to look at Amy. Her eyes were welled up with tears.

"Okay," Amy said bravely. "How do we fix it?"

Emily sighed. "Stall rest for starters. We will have to pack his leg. He should either get a shoe on that foot so there is even pressure on this ankle or the other shoes should come off."

Together Amy and I said, "Other shoes should come off."

Emily nodded. "That would be preferable but I don't know how well he can bear weight on the left foot while you take the other shoes off."

I moaned. "I hadn't thought of that."

"Can we give him a local anesthetic in the ankle?" Amy asked as she bent down to take another look at the x-ray. Julie had snuck from the tack room and had pushed her head under Amy's arm. Amy looked down at the dog and smiled. "You're not supposed to be out here, are you?" Julie looked ashamed but did not budge. She wagged her tail as she stood on her hind legs and licked Amy's face. Amy stroked the dog behind her head and rose. "Let's see what happens."

I looked over at her. "Take them all off?"

She sighed and nodded.

Julie was once again relegated to the tack room while Amy and Emily packed Milton's left ankle. I worked as quickly as I could to pull the remaining shoes off. When we were all done with our tasks, Amy led Milton back to his stall. His limp was not as bad since the local anesthetic had not yet worn off. Amy backed out of the horse stall and stared at her horse. "He is going to have a hard time being alone in the barn when the others are out in the pasture." She contemplated this for a moment and then her face lit up. "I think I'll make a tape recording of the other horses and play it while they are away so he won't get too stressed out."

Emily looked doubtful but then she shrugged. "It might work."

"How are you going to get the other horses to make enough noise?" I asked.

Amy grinned, "Oh they all sing for their breakfast. I'll just have to remember to bring the tape recorder down to the barn with me in the morning."

Julie stuck her head out of the tack room and moaned.

"What is she alerting you to this time?" I wondered.

"She has to go to the bathroom," Amy answered as she waved Julie out of the tack room. Julie bolted out the barn door.

* * *

Chapter 5

I was due back at the farm in two weeks to shoe the other three horses and trim the Pony's feet. Bill, the Pony, was by far the most difficult to handle. Amy had showed me a picture of him from the day she brought him home. He was a rescue, like all the animals on the farm. Bill looked like a bobble-head doll. He was so skinny you couldn't see his flanks past his large head. He still bore the scars from abuse, both physical and mental.

I pulled down the driveway and spotted Amy's brother repairing fences. There were several pieces of the bottom rung missing. I pulled alongside him and rolled down my window. "Hey. Need any help?"

"Nope," he replied without taking his eyes off the fence. As I started to pull away I heard him mutter "Damn Pony."

As I was backing down the barn drive I spotted Bill the Pony grazing by the swing set and it made me chuckle. Clearly, Bill had learned how to escape pasture.

I could hear the comforting noises of horses nickering and sputtering from outside the barn.

The puppy had grown quite a bit in just two weeks. She greeted me at the barn entrance with a riding boot in her mouth. I heard the fast shuffle of her owner attempting to catch up to the young dog. As Amy rounded a corner Julie took off running toward the driveway. The pup stopped and turned toward her out-of-breath mother. The blond tail wagged with glee as her front feet danced. Amy halted in the barn doorway, exasperated. As she brushed her hair from her face she muttered, "Pain in the ass," then she turned and stomped back into the barn. As I followed I looked over my shoulder. Julie's tail was limp and she looked hurt. I did an about turn and met Julie in the driveway. Unsure of me, she dropped the boot and backed away. I leaned down to her and patted her as I retrieved the boot. The dog's ears perked up as I raised the boot over my shoulder and threw it. She leapt and danced toward the boot and grabbed it in her jaws. She trotted back to me and just as I was going to repeat this action I heard grumbling coming from the barn.

"Really? You're going to encourage the incorrigible?" She cleared her throat and glared at me.

I started to carry the boot back into the barn, but when I reached out to hand it to Amy, Julie swooped under my arm and instead of the boot grabbed my glove right off my hand. She ran around outside in big circles, glancing my way occasionally as if to invite me to chase her. "Serves you right!" Amy snorted as she took the boot from me and tossed it in the tack room.

Amy came back to the barn entrance and leaned against the doorframe. "Well? How are you gonna get your glove?"

I puffed out my chest, "Well, I am NOT going to chase her. I hear you tell people yourself that chasing a dog is counterproductive. She will get tired and come back here." I peered outside. I looked at Amy. She was grinning. "Okay. Wait," she said as she turned back to the interior of the barn. She laughed wholeheartedly as she walked down the aisle toward the horses. I looked outside to see where Julie was. Still runnin', no sign of being tired. But she had dropped my glove somewhere because she was now wrestling with a soccer ball. Hmmm.

"You look exhausted," I observed. Another glare.

Amy was down the barn aisle near Hammlet's stall and then she swung around and pointed her finger at me. "It so happens that Julie gets her third or fourth wind around two in the morning. She runs circles in the bedroom and banks off of walls, one of them being behind my bed. So just in case you didn't get the imagery right, she flies over my head and bounces off of the wall above my head. I cannot get any sleep! I have never had a puppy like this, and I have had a lot of puppies! She is impossible!" Amy paused to take a breath and I smiled. Julie was now sitting next to Amy as she finished her rampage.

"No glove." I observed.

"No problem. Watch this. She can track." The woman slapped the side of her leg and Julie fell in next to her step for step.

Amy paused in front of me and held out her hand. "Give me the other glove."

"Uh. No." I replied.

"C'mon. You'll get it back," she pushed.

"I am smarter than I look. Julie already stole one of my gloves and lost it. How stupid do you think I am?"

"I will assume that is a rhetorical question." She said. "Look at it this way. One glove doesn't do you any good. So in the worst possible scenario you lose both gloves and I buy you another pair.

Best case scenario, Julie finds your missing glove. What do you have to lose?"

Had to admit she had a point so I handed over the other glove. Julie leapt in the air, trying to snag my glove before the transaction was complete. Amy was firm with her "No" and Julie immediately sat down and put on her most contrite face. After only a few seconds Amy grinned and then Julie's face was once again beaming with a grin. Amy held the glove under Julie's nose, then pretended to throw the glove, quickly pocketing it in her back pocket.

"Find it," Amy encouraged Julie. Julie stared at Amy as if the owner was an idiot. "Find it" Amy said again pointing out the door. Still nothing. Further encouraging Julie, Amy repeated "Find it," added a hand gesture, and took steps outside of the door. Julie's face lit up as she jumped forward and pulled the second glove from Amy's pocket. The dog then proceeded to race outside, tossing the soft leather up in the air and catching it again. I glared at Amy. She grinned sheepishly. "Oops." Amy was beginning to blush from embarrassment when Julie trotted toward us then dropped the glove at Amy's feet. Amy pulled a treat from her pocket and said, "GOOD girl."

I shook my head with annoyance. "You reward her for that?"

Amy started to bend down. "Sure. She did what I asked. I'm the idiot for doing it wrong."

I opened my mouth to criticize her but didn't get a word out before Amy exclaimed, "Well, lookee here!"

She held out both of my gloves. Amy and I both stared down at Julie, who was in a proper sit, dusting the ground with exuberant wagging of her tail, a proud grin on her face.

"Well, I'll be a monkey's uncle." I said as I took my now damp gloves from Amy's clutches.

Julie leapt up unexpectedly and grabbed the gloves again. This time the game was cut short by Amy's brother Mike, who was walking toward the barn. Julie ran up to show him her prizes and he gave her a pat on the head and said, "Okay, drop it." And Julie did.

Amy and I exchanged glances. "Hmph," she huffed as she turned back into the interior of the barn.

I couldn't help but smile as Mike strutted toward me. "How ya doin'?" I asked. Mike shoved my gloves against my chest and gave me a polite nod as he passed. Julie followed to the barn and immediately looked for her mother. She sat in the middle of the carpeted aisle way as Amy finally pulled Hammlet from his stall. Julie continued to just sit in the aisle way and Amy looked down at the pretty dog. Julie grinned, and thumped her tail on the carpet. Then Amy barked and both Julie and I jumped. But Julie retreated into the tack room as she was trained to do.

Amy is a strange woman.

Mike walked by me a second time, wood rail under his arm, and toward the broken fence. Enough of this funny business; I felt ready to get to work. It wasn't until then that I noticed a figure hiding in the tack room. As Amy led Hammlet toward me I asked in a whisper, "Who is in the tack room?"

Amy stood on her toes to see over the horses back. "Oh. That's Jeff. I didn't know he was here already."

"Who's Jeff?"

"Another farm hand, he says he has worked on cow farms most of his life. Kris is going to start training him today. He had two references. They haven't gotten back to me yet, though. He said that he got fired because he didn't work fast enough."

We both glanced at Jeff through the tack room window. He was holding his right hand in front of his face, examining it. I nodded and smiled, "I can see that."

Jeff strolled up and down the aisle way, reaching out to pat horses as he passed them. It sounded as if he was humming to himself. Amy and I exchanged glances. She shrugged.

Kris came in the barn, chipper. "Hey you two," she greeted us. "Hey Ron."

I looked at her. "Wasn't I included in the 'two'?"

Kris smiled. "No, I meant Amy and Julie."

"Hmm. I always think of them as one," I replied.

Kris looked over her shoulder at Jeff, and then turned toward Amy. "Is that the trainee?"

Amy answered, "No. This poor guy can't afford to go to the zoo so I let him come to the barn and visit with the animals here."

"Ha ha. Funny." Kris turned toward Jeff and marched over. The training began.

We allowed Jeff to lead Hammy back to his stall and retrieve Lucy. We watched impatiently while he struggled with the halter. Lucy glanced at Amy and rolled her eyes. "Uh oh," Amy said as she briskly walked toward the horse.

I watched as Amy took over. "Stand against the other wall while I move her please."

Jeff plastered himself against the wall rather dramatically. Amy led Lucy toward me and I saw the horse kick behind her as she passed Jeff.

"What was that about?" I asked as I took Lucy from Amy.

40

"Lucy can get pretty pissy with people she thinks are idiots. I can already tell you that this will be a problem. She has decided she doesn't like Jeff. So unless he is a fantastic horse handler…"

We looked over at Jeff, as Kris watched him with annoyance while he demonstrated hopping on one foot, patting his head while he rubbed his stomach. "Like this?" he asked Kris.

We heard Kris say, "No. That is not what I meant when I said multi-tasking."

The phone rang and Kris jumped to get it. "Wait here," she told Jeff. She gave Amy a dirty look as she swung the door to the tack room open further. Julie watched Kris with interest. The dog walked over to the cookie jar and stared at it. Hint, hint. Kris replaced the phone and walked toward Amy. I heard them whisper, but couldn't make out what was being said.

Jeff strolled over to Amy. "You wanted to see me."

"Yes. Why were you fired from the cattle farms?"

Jeff blushed. This had my interest now, so I placed Lucy's hind foot on the ground and snuck closer so I could eavesdrop.

"Uhhhh." Jeff started to stammer.

Amy shook her head. "You lied. You said you didn't work fast enough and that is why you were fired. Was it because you were too busy fondling the cows?"

"Uh. Well, uh."

"Get out of here. NOW!" she snapped.

Jeff hightailed it out of the barn. He returned about two minutes later. "Can anyone give me a ride home? My ride won't be here for..."

Amy took a quick step toward him. "OUT!" She pointed toward the door. *"Now!!!"*

Jeff turned and ran. When I turned toward Lucy again she had a huge grin on her face.

Kris walked over to us. "He wouldn't have worked out anyway. He was as dumb as a box of rocks, but not as good looking."

* * *

Chapter 6

Over time Milton's fracture healed and he was once again permitted to join his friends in pasture. It was time to get shoes on him again before he tore up his feet. Again, I was running ahead of schedule. An earlier appointment had canceled. I wasn't sure if I should bother to arrive at Amy's farm early because if she were not home I would have to wait for her, or her assistant, to be present. I drove through the drive-through of a Hardy's restaurant, picked up lunch and headed on to the Barnum Road farm. There was a gazebo by the pond where I planned to eat lunch. When I arrived I couldn't help but notice how quiet the farm was. I passed the horses in a pasture beside the drive. Lucy, the mare, lifted her head to stare at me as I drove by.

It was rather serene until Julie raced by the truck, carrying what looked like a fish in her mouth. Amy wasn't far behind, running, yelling and waving her arms. Julie passed my truck, ducked under a fence and rounded the pond. Amy came to a staggering halt by my passenger side window. I rolled down the window and noticed that sweat was trickling down the side of her face. I couldn't help but smile. "How long had you been chasing her?" I asked.

Amy bent at the waist and placed her hands on her knees, trying to catch her breath. "That is her sixth time around the pond." She gasped.

Now I was full out laughing. "Why do you chase her?"

"I figured if I kept her moving she wouldn't be able to stop, drop the fish, and roll all over it. I had hoped I could tire her out too. I am going to have to give her a third bath today! She is impossible. Worst puppy I have ever had!"

I was still laughing as I watched Julie on the other side of the pond. Yep, she was definitely rolling in something and I didn't think it was clover.

Amy watched me watch her dog in amusement. Instead of an argument she said, "Are you going to let me in your truck or do I have to jump on the back bumper?"

I reached over and pushed the door open. We didn't speak during the ride down the driveway. I couldn't suppress my grin and Amy frowned as she watched her dog from the window. In a low voice I heard her mutter, "Pain in the ass."

After an hour of silence, while I replaced shoes on Milton, Julie raced into the barn. She came to a skidding stop that unfurled the carpet. When she came to a complete halt, Julie jumped on her owner with (I hoped) muddy paws. Amy threw her hands up, Milton jumped in the air and landed on my foot and I fell. Julie sat quietly, taking in the scene, looking at all of us as if we were nuts. I must admit I muttered, "Pain in the ass." That did get a smile out of Amy.

When Julie spotted Milton she hung her head. "Fun over," she seemed to say.

She diligently pushed her way into the tack room, circled five or six times and lay down. Her head was still peeking through the door and she expended a huge sigh that sounded more like "garumph."

In an attempt to break the awkward silence that so often passed between Amy and me, I innocently asked, "Did you get a chance to see the movie *Marley & Me?*"

When I didn't hear any reply, I looked over my shoulder to see Amy glaring at me. "Are you implying something?"

I stammered a bit. "Uh, nope. Just askin'. I saw the movie and thought it was pretty funny."

"We saw it. I enjoyed the book, but the movie, not so much. I found it annoying, frankly."

I chuckled. "A little too close to home?"

"Uh. I don't THINK so! Are you comparing Julie to Marley? Or me to the owners? Because if you are I will let you know that THEY went to some crappy, parking lot trainer, were kicked out of class and quit. They didn't make any effort to educate themselves so they could train their dog properly. It wasn't the dog's fault, but I would never live in a house with a dog that behaved that badly. I have been working with a behaviorist, Greta Marchus, who is helping ME become educated on canine physiology, psychology, and instincts in order to channel it all into a training method that suits Julie."

I stood up and stretched my back for a moment. "Okay, okay. Don't get your panties in a bunch." As soon as the words were out of my mouth I regretted saying them. I slowly turned my head to look at Amy's face. She was fuming.

"I am about to give you a piece of my mind, Ron Bowling!"

I couldn't help myself. "Oh no, not your last one." Crap. I looked over again toward Amy. I couldn't see her right away because Milton's head was in the way. The horse was looking at me as if I were an idiot, contemplating making a run for it. When Milton straightened his neck I could see tears streaming down Amy's face. "Oh shit." I felt bad and started walking toward the crying woman. Then I stopped because I realized she was laughing so hard she was crying. Sure is hard to figure her out.

Amy glanced at the clock above the tack room door. "Whoa. I didn't know how late it was," she said.

Before I could inquire a man walked through the barn doors. "I am here to fill out an application." He explained.

Amy nodded. "Hold on," she said, disappearing into the tack room. She returned to the doorway clutching a clipboard, standing over her immobile dog in a straddle. "You can fill this out and we can talk when you are done."

The guy glanced at Julie, staring up adoringly at Amy. "Nice dog. Does she do any tricks?"

"Some," Amy answered as she used hand signals to instruct Julie to spin in a circle (couldn't have been hard to teach), bow, and rub her paws over her face as if she was ashamed. *I* didn't even know Julie could do that.

"Wow. What's your secret?"

Without a reply Amy returned to Milton and spoke soothingly to him. Soon her noises sounded like a monotone hum. "What are you doing?" I asked, without taking my eyes off what I was doing. Amy replied, "I know it sounds bad but he seems to calm down with a one tone hum. I guess it's like white noise to him."

"It doesn't do much for me."

46

Before Amy could respond with a sarcastic quip I heard another voice say "Done." Milton started to get jittery again so I placed his foot on the ground, stroked his flank, and waited. I leaned against the wall while Amy and the man discussed the job position available. "You have here that you have experience with horses and dogs," she read from the clipboard. She looked up and the guy nodded. "We got ourselves a huntin' dog tied in back. My neighbor has horses and sometimes I see him ridin' him."

Amy opened her mouth to reply but he continued.

"By the way, can you have somebody pick me up for work and take me home and stuff?" He stuck his index finger half way up his nose with one hand and adjusted his crotch with the other.

Amy and I stared at this guy for a beat or two before we broke into laughter.

The guy extracted his finger from his nose, examined what he had on his finger. "What?" he asked, looking between both of us.

I coughed out another laugh then said, "She'll let you know."

The man nodded his head. "Good, good. Hope to hear from you soon. Don't call too late 'cause I got five kids and we like'em to git ta bed early."

Amy was fighting to suppress more laughter so she simply nodded. Thirty seconds later she leaned to glance out the door. She burst out laughing again, "He's gone."

I chuckled and returned to Milton, "But waiting for your call."

"Why did you say that?"

"To get him out of here, one. Two, with your track record he may end up being your best candidate."

"If it wouldn't upset my horse, I'd slap you." Then I heard her groan. "Here comes another one."

I heard boots scuff on the carpet as contestant number two entered. Amy repeated the same process except this time, when she entered the tack room, Julie stood up and wagged her tail at her. I finished Milton's feet and walked him back to his stall. He practically jumped through the open door and sprang at his full hay rack.

Amy was already speaking with the second applicant when I returned to the wash stall with a broom. She was just dismissing him as I started to sweep. I waited for a polite minute then asked, "What was wrong with that one?"

"He wanted me to pay him under the table so he could avoid paying child support."

I continued sweeping but looked up at her. "But you do pay under the table."

She shrugged and snapped, "First, I hire 1099 employees, or try to. Second, if we ever had anyone work here long enough to report them on payroll we would. Kris is on payroll, for example. But, that's not the point. Those are his kids. If he doesn't take care of THEM how am I supposed to trust him to take care of MINE?"

With all of the horses out of the way Julie sidled up to Amy. Amy smiled and bent over to kiss the dog just below the dog's nose. She whispered something to Julie.

"Are you talking about me?" I accused.

"No, egomaniac. I am discussing my problems with Julie. I tell her all of my secrets." Amy smiled and rubbed Julie behind her ear then added, "She is my secret keeper. Can't trust anyone else with the stuff that runs through MY head."

I was nodding in agreement when I saw a blond blur race out the barn door. I looked around and realized that Julie was following Amy, and Amy left. Guess the conversation was over. Rude.

* * *

Chapter 7

I was in a great mood, on my way to Barnum Road, on a nice sunny Spring afternoon. When I got out of the truck to open the gate at the end of the drive I heard birds chirping, and could hear the rustle of woodland creatures shuffling to safety in the woods. I pulled into the drive and spotted Amy and all of her dogs out on a small dock. Feeling rather casual, I sauntered to the dock. Amy was tossing flat rocks into the pond around the dock. "Uh, what are you doing?" I asked. She jumped and the dogs started to bark.

"You scared the crap out of me!" she scolded.

"Sorry. I didn't mean to sneak up on you. Great watch dogs by the way."

"We were having a relaxing afternoon until you got here."

"I think those rocks are a tad big to skip across the pond surface."

Amy rolled her eyes at me. "I am placing rocks around the edge of the dock so that when we are swimming our feet don't get stuck in the muck. It creeps me out."

I stepped forward with outstretched arms. "Let me help. I like throwing things."

We stood quietly tossing large, flat rocks into the water. It was very peaceful, until Julie spotted me. She must have been exploring in the woods when I arrived because my presence seemed to be a surprise. She came barreling down the dock, and as I turned to greet her she leapt into the air. She landed on my chest and I started to fall backwards into the water. To save myself I instinctively grabbed onto whatever was available. Amy. We both tumbled into the water. As I was rising to the surface I saw Julie, midair! She landed between her owner and me but then she proceeded to circle us so we couldn't move. Amy and I were both getting frustrated. She turned to me and we chanted together, "Pain in the ass." Amy fumbled in her pockets and came up with a soggy pack of cigarettes. "Those won't do us any good," I groused.

"Just watch." She said. Amy tossed the pack onto the lawn and Julie couldn't help herself, she followed. As we both crawled out of the water Julie brought the pack of cigarettes to Amy.

"She is a retriever, after all." I snickered.

Another eye roll.

We stood outside for a while, drying off. The wind had picked up and it had become a little chilly, so we weren't completely dry as we headed to the barn. The dogs were frolicking innocently by the pond when we left them, except for Julie. She was still planted by her aggravated owner's side.

It took several hours to get all the horses trimmed and shoed. When Amy went into the tack room to get her wallet she exited with a concerned look. "Where is Julie?" she asked.

I looked around. I didn't have any luck finding the pooch. Amy walked outside of the barn and started to call Julie. As I joined her, my attention was drawn to a woman hurrying down the drive, Julie at her heels.

"I think there is something wrong with your dog!" she exclaimed.

Amy made a face and replied, "No shit. She runs off, rolls in crap, and jumps on people….."

The woman interrupted. "No. Your other dog. Your black dog."

Amy glanced around as if she would find answers. "What do you mean? They were all outside and we are fenced in with a gate."

The woman shook her head. "Your gate is open. The wind probably blew it that way. I was jogging and your dogs were following me. I decided to turn around and bring them home because I know you try to keep them close. Anyway, when I turned around I saw one of your black dogs stagger onto the lawn and collapse. I hate to say this, but I think she is dead…"

The end of the sentence was probably not heard by Amy as she muttered "Joanie" under her breath and took off running, at an incredible pace, in bare feet, up the gravel drive. I followed her, Julie at my heels, and when I caught up I could see her standing about ten feet away from her dead dog. She took a deep breath, walked over and picked up her dog. She turned and started walking toward me with eyes welled with tears. She didn't speak. She just walked past me, back to her farm, with her dog in her arms. I again followed at a respectful distance until we got closer to the house and she laid Joanie gently under a tree. I walked to her side and looked down at the peaceful dog. Suddenly Amy exclaimed, "I don't know what to do! What do I do? I have never had any of my dogs just drop dead! I usually cremate them and we bury them in the pet cemetery." She started to pace. "Where do I take her? What am I going to do?"

I looked at my watch. "It is 6:00. Most vet offices are already closed."

"A vet? A vet? Don't you think she is a tad beyond a vet? What do you want me to do, take her to a vet just to screw with them?"

I am stuttering now. "No. I just mean they usually arrange for cremation, don't they?"

She sat down next to her dog and stroked Joanie's head. I felt helpless.

Amy shook her head. "I can't leave her outside all night. I don't think it is right to keep her in the house, do you? Isn't that a little creepy? I just don't know what to do."

Just then we were both distracted by the vocal stylings of very loud ducks. Amy glanced over her shoulder at the intruders. She sighed. "Julie probably chased those ducks over here from Mrs. Campbell's farm down the street." She stood abruptly and asked, in a panicked tone, "Oh my God, where is Julie?"

"Well, how many ducks did YOU see?" I asked.

"Two," she snapped.

"No. There is one duck and a yellow lab swimming after it."

She swung around and gasped. "Oh my God! Well, I know she is a good swimmer." Then she laughed too hard, almost hysterically.

I volunteered to dig an appropriate hole to bury Joanie. Amy directed me to the pet cemetery where, frankly, I was a little nervous about digging. Amy wrapped a beautiful comforter around Joanie and placed her in the hole. We both stood back and just stared at the bundled dogs' figure for a moment. It was very tranquil for a moment. Suddenly a census taker barged around the corner of the house and started asking questions. I put my hands in the air. "Hey, I don't live here."

I watched Amy's facial expression change from sad and loving to hatred. She slowly turned and yelled at the man for the intrusion. "Do you see us standing around a freshly dug hole? By the way, what in hell do you think you are doing prancing around the entire property? You ring a bell. Nobody answers, you leave! This is private property and frankly, I have NO problem asking my friend to dig another hole!"

The man stood frozen for a moment. At least until Amy wrestled the shovel from my grasp and chased the man to his car. I have known her for a year now, and knowing her the way I do, I think she used great restraint.

I gracefully took my leave after I returned the shovel to the tool shed. As I was walking somberly to my truck Julie ran up to me, soaking wet, with a duck clutched in her jaws. "Oh. Your owner isn't going to like this." As I pulled myself into my truck I muttered to myself, "Wouldn't want to be her in five minutes." As I started to back out of the barn drive I spotted Amy, arms wrapped around Julie, duck on the lawn.

* * *

Chapter 8

I returned from vacation to a snarling answering machine message. "You're fired," Amy snapped.

"What?" I asked nobody as I walked toward the phone. I picked up the phone and dialed the farm.

"Hello?" Amy answered.

"Hey. It's Ron. I got a strange message…"

She cut me off. "I called and called and you never showed up to do the horse's feet. I hired somebody else. Somebody reliable."

"Wait a minute," I said, almost pleading. I had become very attached to those horses. "They aren't due until next week."

"That may be true but both Hammlet and Milton lost shoes. They are thoroughbreds. They have thin soles. They need to have shoes on! But if you're going to go off on vacations..."

I cut her off. "That is my first vacation in ten years."

"Well the new guy says he always has other Farriers on call when he is away." She hung up.

Geez, I thought to myself as I ran my hands through my hair. I pulled a diet soda from the refrigerator, sat in my Lazyboy chair and stared at the ceiling for about a minute. Bitch.

Months went by and I had a rare Sunday off. I decided to take the risk of rejection and call Amy once again. I had hoped that her temper had cooled with time. It took quite a while for somebody to answer the phone. The voice of a child answered, "Hello?"

"Hi is a, your, a …is Amy there?" I inquired.

I then noticed that the young girl sounded out of breath. "I am sorry. We are waiting for the vet. Amy is in the front pasture with Lucy. Lucy is hurt."

"What's wrong?" my voice raised in alarm.

"I dunno but it is worse than the horses at the race track."

"I'm not sure what that means."

She coughed then answered. "The horses at the race track don't run just because they get a scratch."

Trying to stifle a laugh I said my good-byes and hung up. Then I headed to the farm on Barnum Road.

As I drove I negotiated with myself. What if I am not welcome there? The vet should surely arrive before I do. Is this really any of my business? I drove faster as these thoughts passed through my mind. Lucy was a beautiful, Chestnut (Red) mare. It took me months to gain her trust after the previous bad experiences that she had. The other Farrier must have been an idiot, not knowing much about horses. I realized on my first visit that Lucy had a tipped pelvis. You cannot lift her legs too high. She cannot tolerate it. I kept myself preoccupied with my thoughts until I reached Barnum Road. As I turned into the drive I could see Lucy in the front pasture, Amy by her side, holding her left front leg in the air. I could tell that moving her would be challenging. As I pondered what could be wrong it hit me. Amy lost her last horse to a broken leg. Amy must be terrified. I felt afraid as well.

I pushed the gate open with my truck and entered. I pulled along the fence line and parked. I hopped the pasture fence and rushed out to examine Lucy. Amy didn't say a thing at first. Behind my truck, her brother Mike parked his truck. He climbed the fence and sauntered out to greet us. As he approached us he shook his head, "Why do they always get injured in the farthest point of the pasture?"

I looked around and spotted the other horses. I examined Lucy's left leg. "She has a bowed tendon."

"How do you know?" Amy asked.

I drew her to the side of Lucy and showed her where the tendon had bowed.

"She can walk into the barn," I stated.

"I'm not sure if she should. What if the injury gets worse?"

Mike looked around and said, "Don't see much choice."

I gathered the other horses and started to lead them toward the barn. Sure enough, Lucy followed them. I kept the boys at a slow pace so Lucy would put as little stress on the injured tendon as possible. As we were closing in on the barn the vet, Emily, slowly glided down the drive in her truck.

After a full examination the vet concurred with my finding.

"We have to change her shoes," Emily stated.

"Glad I'm here," I replied.

Amy turned to walk toward the tack room and muttered, "So am I." When she opened the tack room door Julie sprang out anxiously. "Oh, I am SO sorry Julie." Amy pointed to the exit and Julie ran outside for a potty break.

I looked over at Amy. "Now I know why you looked different in the pasture."

She squinted, "Why?"

"You didn't have Julie by your side."

Amy smiled, "She is my best feature, that's for sure." Then she started to rifle through a tack box for pain relievers for Lucy.

"By the way, you are un-fired."

* * *

Chapter 9

The next night I phoned the farm to check up on Lucy. A bowed tendon is very painful and there is a great deal of stall rest and therapy required to pull a horse through it. Many people put their horses down if they bow a tendon. I knew that wouldn't occur to Amy. Emily knew it too, or at least she knew better than to bring it up. This would probably cause Amy to remain in Ohio throughout the summer as opposed to traveling to the family home in Ontario.

As soon as Amy answered the phone I regretted calling. She sounded perturbed. Not the best hour to phone, I guess.

Amy sighed and told me that she was just exasperated with Julie's energy level. "She learns everything easily but I cannot calm her down."

"Still banking off the walls, huh?"

"Yep! She also climbs up the ladder to the slide. She slides down and then leaps over the swings. I have to find a positive way to channel her energy. Maybe I should get a dog sled and make her take me to run errands. Just kidding. She also needs mental stimulation."

"I know you're kidding about the dog sled, but there has to be some kind of dog sport she could do," I suggested. "Not sure what kind of mental stimulation a dog would need though."

"Well, she gets bored easily. Her crate was in the dog gym, so at dinner I put her in the small washroom on the first floor. I took up the small carpet and the toilet paper. There was NOTHING in sight she could have gotten into. I always let her out while her sisters are finishing their food so if she tries to steal food from them they will correct her. After all there are some lessons that she can only learn from another dog."

I added, "I have seen you show your teeth and growl at her if she tries to jump up and take your food."

"Well, yeah," she admitted. "It cannot be the same though. Anyway, I opened the washroom door and she had climbed on top of the toilet seat, up to the sink, and got the medicine cabinet open."

"Oh no!" I exclaimed. "Did she get into anything that could hurt her?"

"We only keep, or kept, little hotel soaps, shampoos and stuff like that in there. Although the small bottle of mouthwash could have killed her, if she had gotten into it. I don't see how she could have balanced on the edge of the seat to pull the cabinet open with her paw without falling backwards."

Thoughtfully I said, "Well she is obviously agile…."

"That is funny that you used that word. I just found something about dog agility. And it is a timed event. I am on a website now watching a video of some woman running a Dalmatian through an obstacle course. It looks pretty easy. I bet any idiot could do this!"

She seemed to be talking more to herself at that point and I heard typing on the other end of the line. I was about to ring off when I heard her say, "Oh my God!"

"What?" I answered, grinning to myself. Amy missed the joke and said, "I just heard a horrible crash!"

I lowered my voice. "Are you alone, Clarisse?" I asked.

"That's not really funny. I am, though. My brother is at work and Ty is with her Mom."

"I wasn't suggesting that your seven year old niece could protect you."

Amy snapped at me, "I don't need protection."

I didn't say anything for a moment.

Then Amy asked in a softer voice, "But would you mind staying on the phone with me while I go check things out outside?"

I knew laughing would royally piss her off and she'd probably hang up so I used self-restraint. I can always rib her about it later, another day, when I know she is safe. "Sure."

"I'm not going to talk, okay? If somebody is out here I don't want them to hear me coming."

I agreed. Then I remembered that moron that put an ad in the paper trying to recruit help in doing her harm. I suggested that she call the police. Her whisper was barely audible as she replied, "I got a gun."

"Did you take any of the dogs with you?" I persisted.

Still whispering, but more irritated now, "No. I'm not going to put my dogs out if there is danger. I protect THEM, not the other way around." She fell just short of calling me an idiot. Then her voice rose back to normal. "Christ. That idiot that works, I mean worked, here ran over the gate at the end of the drive."

"It's attached to posts that are anchored by concrete. How is that even possible?"

Amy growled. "She always complained about being required to get out of her car to open the gate and then get out of her car, again, to close it."

"But it was like that when she showed up for the interview."

"I know but it is cold outside. She obviously decided, screw me and my rules, and grinded into the ground." Empathetically I snarled, "I hope her car is seriously damaged."

Amy's voice became more alert. "Orrrr. She may have done something wrong in the barn and was making her escape."

I could hear Amy panting a bit as her footfalls became faster. The sound of the barn doors sliding emanated through the phone, then the tack room doors opening. I heard her moan.

"What? What did she do? Or not do? Are the horses okay?" I asked urgently.

"She stole my saddles. Bitch."

"Were they expensive?"

"Do you know anything about the horse world or are you just a guy that likes to play with horses?"

"A little of both I guess."

"The four of them were worth about $4-5000 each."

I whistled.

Her mood changed quickly. I could hear the horses nickering in the background and the sound of the treat jar being unscrewed. Hammy's hungry noises were the loudest. "Oh well. I can eventually replace them. I'll buy some of those fabric saddles to school in. The good ones will have to remain in the house under lock and key."

"You don't sound that upset now," I observed.

"It's just stuff."

"So true," I added as I felt my eyelids start to get heavy.

"Okay." She said. "It is 9 o'clock and all is well. I'll let you go now."

"Wait," I yelled into the phone. "What about Lucy. How is Lucy?"

"Oh. I wondered why you called. She is great. It is hard for her to be on stall rest, though. I got more videos for her to watch but she isn't having it."

"As long as she seems to be comfortable."

"I am watching her nod her head up and down for another cookie and she seems like her usual self. Satisfied?"

"Yep. That's all I wanted to hear."

* * *

Chapter 10

Seasons change very quickly in Ohio. The snow covered the small farm in a crisp, sparkling blanket. I could see tracks from where the dogs ran. The pond was also covered with the white stuff. It made the acreage look bigger, as if it went on forever.

I spotted Amy, with Julie at her side, trudging down to the barn to meet me. They headed inside to refuge from the winter as I parked my truck. When I entered, I passed a woman wiping down the woodwork in the barn. We exchanged "Hi's" as I moved by. I looked around for Amy and Julie, and I noticed the horse arena doors were open.

"We're in here," I heard Amy shout.

I stepped into the arena and there were obstacles all over. Jumps, some kind of teeter-totter, poles that wavered, (I later learned they are called weave poles), and many jumps. As I stood gaping at all of the equipment Amy called out, with childlike glee, "Watch what she can do."

I watched as Julie executed all the obstacles with perfection. Well, other than the weave poles.

I applauded as Amy and Julie finished the course. They were both grinning as they approached me. "Julie and I took agility classes last fall," she explained as she looked over the arena. "I am obviously going to build her a gym of her own. She can't keep running in here, it gets too cold. Plus it's a pain to move the stuff around so the horses don't get into it."

"I'm impressed. *Julie* looked like she knew what she was doing, but…"

Amy chuckled. "I know. I am her biggest handicap."

"So, the big question…is she less energetic? Or as you put it, less a 'pain in the ass'?"

"She is much, much better, unless she spots a woodland critter."

"Ahhh. Those woodland critters. That's a pesky habit to break. It's just so ingrained in them."

Amy sighed. "I know. But I figure eventually we'll be all out of woodland critters." She grinned as she headed back into the barn.

When we were finished, Amy turned the horses out into the arena, after she picked up Julie's toys. I looked over the calendar to schedule my next visit. As I was circling a date Amy reappeared. "I'll have to ask Kris to come in that day. Julie and I have our first agility tournament, Thursday through Saturday."

"Oh really? Where?" I asked.

"At the IX center, they have the Crown Classic."

"THAT is going to be your first show?"

Amy shrugged. "Sure, why not?"

I left shaking my head in awe of her bravery or naiveté.

Julie retreated to the tack room as I pulled Milton from his stall. As we were walking by the woman with the damp rags I said, "Be careful. He has a nervous disorder."

She looked over at us then jumped out, waving her hands and yelled "Boo!"

Milton reared up and extricated himself from my grasp. He took off running out of the barn doors. Amy grabbed what looked like a marracca instrument and was out the door after Milton. I glared at the woman as I turned toward Milton's stall to retrieve a lead rope.

I was only a few feet outside of the barn when Amy returned, clutching Milton's halter.

"That was fast," I complimented. Amy held up the marracca. "When you shake it, it sounds like grain in a feed scoop. Can you grab me some treats so I can reward him?"

The woman guffawed. "Reward him for what? He ran away."

Amy turned to her and said, "You're fired. If you are standing here after I put Milton in the wash stall I am going to slap the skin off of your face."

Amy was speaking calmly, almost softly. I wondered why until I realized she didn't want Milton to get further upset.

The woman and I passed in the tack room door. I was exiting with cookies, and she was entering to get her purse. She glanced through the window and saw Amy moving Milton into the wash stall so she sped up her pace and ran out of the barn.

I was patting Milton. "You know, let's put him back in his stall for a while, and let him relax. Get me Lucy."

Amy nodded. "Good idea."

"You know, I have to ask. How many potential employees have you gone through? Are they all idiots?"

Amy smiled a bit. "To answer your first question, 23. Every once in a while we get somebody worthwhile. They may last a year or two then they burn out. Otherwise, yes, they are all idiots."

"23? That's a lot. How long have you lived here?"

"5 years."

"Geesh. I wouldn't have believed it if I didn't see it. Kris is a keeper, though, right?"

"Sure. She went to Lake Erie College and was in the Equine program. She did her internship here and decided to stay on."

"Wow. You do have slim pickin's in this area."

We heard a car pull down the drive. Kris got out and walked toward the barn. She called to Amy, "Is the trainee here yet?" as she looked around the drive.

"Already gone," Amy called back.

Kris shook her head, did an about turn and headed back to her car.

* * *

Chapter 11

© 2010 www.PawPrintsLife.com

I was sweeping the barn floor of hoof shavings and discarded pieces of nail when Julie bounded through the barn door. When she spotted me she spun around, ran straight at me and leapt. I staggered backwards and struggled to stay upright as Julie wiggled in my arms. She licked my face as I held her. Amy marched into the barn behind her. She took in the scene and laughed. I placed Julie on the floor and she ran circles around me. I looked up at Amy. "You look pissed."

Amy nodded. "I asked the guy that was working here, Gary…"

I cut her off. "What? You found someone to work here?"

Amy smiled, "He's been here for five weeks. I called him to tell him I'd be later than I thought. Would he let the dogs out to go potty?"

"Uh oh. He didn't?"

Amy shook her head. "No. He did. But he didn't put them back in the house. When I was driving down the street I had to collect them from neighbors' yards. Debbie was very close to the busy street."

"Did you call the guy and ask him what his problem was?"

Amy nodded, "Yep. You won't believe this. He said, 'You didn't say to put them back in the house'," she said in a dumb voice.

I rubbed the back of my head. "Oh geez. What an idiot. Is everyone okay?"

"Yep. Except Gary. I'm gonna killll him."

"I take it he is fired."

"Oh yeah," Amy nodded.

I looked down as Julie spun around me in circles. "Agility isn't helping with her energy level anymore?" I asked.

Amy grimaced. "Not today. She only got to run each course once. It is a very charged environment too. I must admit the sport is much harder than it looks."

I leaned over Julie behind her ear when she came to a halt in front of me. "So? How did it go at the show?"

Amy sighed and slid down a wall to sit on the floor. "Well, when I took all the dogs out this morning to go to the bathroom Julie ran off into the woods and came back muddy. She jumped on me when she returned so now she had mud up to her belly, and I had muddy paw prints all over my clothes. I couldn't find a dolly to carry her crate so I used my niece's skateboard and a lot of bungee cords. When we finally arrived at the IX center Julie and I entered, still covered in mud. I pulled the crate on the skateboard behind me. Funny thing about skateboards is that when weight shifts it goes in another direction. Soooo, we are muddy, moving in a zigzag pattern through the IX center and we pass some people that are putting curlers in their dogs' hair, blow drying their coats, and giving the dogs' pedicures. We got a *lot* of stares."

By now I was laughing. Amy glared at me for a beat then she reluctantly started to laugh along with me. She started to laugh harder and tears glistened in her eyes. She tried to continue the recount of her day. "Then when we got out to the agility ring Julie raced past me, made up her own course, and when she ran out of ideas she threw herself at me like ricochet rabbit. But we did some shopping and shared lunch. It actually really was a great day, just the two of us."

"Were you stuck sitting around the conformation snobs?" I asked.

"Oh NO! As we came to the center of the IX there was a crowd of casually dressed people, playing with their dogs. I thought to myself, 'THESE are my people'. Although there was one bitch. As Julie and I were leaving the jumpers ring, with all the jumps behind us in the down position, she asked sarcastically, "What's your secret?"

"So I guess you aren't going back tomorrow?"

Amy added one more "bitch" under her breath before she pulled herself up from her sitting position. She looked surprised. "Of course we're going back! I have no dignity."

She felt around her pockets and grimaced. "I'm sorry. I left my checkbook in the house. I'll run and get it."

I leaned the broom against the wall of the wash stall. "How 'bout I follow you to the house. I need to use the restroom if that is okay."

"Sure." She turned and led Julie and me to the house. Julie would run past us about 50 feet then turn and run back. She certainly covered more ground than we did on the short walk.

As we entered, the other dogs danced in circles. In all of their excitement only one dog made the faux pas of jumping on me briefly. Amy reached over, grabbed the dog's scruff on the back of her head and pulled her down. "Off, Debbie," Amy said with a sigh. Debbie sat politely in front of me then, tongue hanging out of the side of her mouth. I used the facilities as Amy rifled through the cheque book. As I came out of the powder room she was pulling a cheque free. She reached out to hand it to me as Julie raced by, bearing the end of the toilet paper roll in her mouth, the rest of the roll trailing behind. The other dogs celebrated and the trail of paper broke.

Amy stated the obvious, "You didn't close the door." When she looked at me I was laughing. Hands on hips she said, "Sure it's funny to outsiders. This kind of stuff goes on ALL day and most of the night."

I was still laughing as I pulled away from the barn. I looked in my rearview mirror and I could see the other dogs dancing around Amy and Julie as they headed to the dog gym, inclusive of indoor pool. Julie started to bark as if she was relaying the days' events to her sisters.

I was smiling when I left, which is usually how I judge any event or visit; 'Was I smiling when I left?'

* * *

Chapter 12

I had been at the barn for 30 minutes. I had phoned her cell phone several times but I only got her voicemail. I hesitated, but finally decided to walk to the house and ring the bell. I could hear the dogs barking in the house, but no answer from Amy. The dogs all jumped up in a window, all but Julie. Hmmm, Amy must not be here if Julie isn't.

I hung around for about an hour before I decided to move on to another client's farm. I planned to return later.

While I was shoeing another horse I could hear my cell phone ringing incessantly. Finally, I put the horse back in his stall and accessed my voicemail. The message was from Kris Harper and she sounded out of breath. Amy had to take Julie to the vet. It was an emergency. Kris offered to meet me at the farm. I dialed the phone and Kris picked up right away.

"Hi. It's Ron Bowling. What's going on?"

Kris sounded tearful as she explained that Julie was acting lethargic this morning. Amy rushed her to her vet. Apparently, Julie had been poisoned with a rodenticide and was bleeding out internally. Amy rushed her from her vet to the specialty hospital where Julie was getting blood transfusions. A knot in my stomach tightened with every word Kris uttered. "Is she going to make it?" I choked.

Kris openly started to cry. "I, I don't know."

"Well, I'll be able to get to the farm in about two hours. Will that be okay?"

Kris stuttered, "Y,y,y,yes. I'll be here." I heard her sniffling as she hung up.

It only took me an hour and a half to get back to Barnum Road. Kris had the other dogs outside running around the yard when I arrived. I slammed the door of my truck and walked over to her. Her face was streaked from tears as she tossed a ball with a chuck-it. The dogs turned and raced for the ball. The black lab I know as Linda won the race. She trotted back to Kris with the ball and dropped it at her feet. When Kris ignored her, Linda grabbed the ball and dropped it at my feet. I smiled down at her as I reached down to retrieve the ball. I tossed it toward the house and watched as the girls raced off again. I looked over at Kris. "Any news?"

She shook her head. She cleared her throat. "Amy said that Julie is in intensive care still getting blood transfusions. She may come home to get one of the other girls to be a blood donor."

"Does she know how Julie was poisoned?"

She shrugged. "They don't have ANY poisons on this farm. They don't even use fertilizers on their grass, so it's safe for the horses to eat it." She cleared her throat again. "She thinks maybe a neighbor..."

I raised my eyebrows. "A neighbor...?"

Kris nodded. "I guess Julie took off in the woods again this morning. When Amy spotted her running toward home Julie was trotting down the drive. The guy across the street hates, HATES DOGS. He may have poisoned her. He shot other neighbor's dogs. They warned her about him."

"Uhhh. I don't want to be him when Julie gets better."

"If, If Julie gets better." She said.

"No, WHEN she gets better," I said as I turned toward the barn. "You coming?" I asked over my shoulder.

As I was about to enter the barn I heard a car motoring down the drive. I looked down the drive and spotted Amy's SUV. She stopped halfway down the drive. She stepped out of her car and whistled. The dogs sped to her side. She reached down and hugged the whole group. She pulled Cinder from the group, kissed her on her nose and whispered something in her ear. She told Cinder to stay as Kris called the other girls back. Amy waved at Kris. "I gotta get back," she yelled. As she turned back toward her car, Cinder at her side, she spotted me. She waved before she opened the door for Cinder and the dog leapt into the car. Amy slid in next to the dog, then she looked over her shoulder and started backing back down the drive.

I felt helpless. There is really something special about Julie. I had grown very attached to her. I shook off my worries and entered the barn.

I worked on all of the horses. Kris and I didn't feel like engaging in our usual banter. It was quiet, but I got the job done.

I wasn't smiling when I left.

* * *

Chapter 13

Julie was often in my thoughts; after 17 days I broke down and phoned Amy. I got her voicemail. I went about my days' working, counting the days until I would return to the farm and learn Julie's fate. I was annoyed that nobody thought enough of me to let me know how she was doing.

Finally it was time. The drive to Barnum Road seemed to take forever. My thoughts kept spinning as I drove. What if Julie is gone? What an unbearable day this will be.

I drove slowly down Barnum Road. I hesitated before making the turn into the drive. Finally I took a deep breath and pushed through the gate. When I got out of my truck to close the gate behind me I was attacked by a playful, beautiful, yellow lab. She bounced in the air and grabbed my arm. She then pulled off my left glove and took off running with it. I laughed as I watched her dart away with her new prize. Gloves are easy to come by. Dogs like Julie are not.

The atmosphere in the barn that day was celebratory. Although Julie had to remain in the tack room while the horses were out, every time I walked by the open door and glanced at her she wagged her tail with enthusiasm. She looked great! Finally I had to ask, "Do you know how she was poisoned?"

Amy's facial expression changed from calm to grim. "I think it was the neighbor across the street. If Julie ran over there, through the back woods, he could have given her the poison. Two other neighbors, when we first moved in here, made the effort to come over and warn me about the prick. When I had to go to a zoning meeting to build our dog gym, he showed up and ranted and raved about how dogs are menaces."

I didn't ask the burning question in my mind. I couldn't help but wonder how she was going to handle it. Then she continued. "I went to the Sherriff's office to file a criminal complaint. They told me I should take care of it myself. Can you believe that? I was trying to do the law abiding thing…"

"So what are you going to do?"

"I dunno. I filed a claim in small claims court but that isn't very satisfying."

"Well I want to go on record. I was not happy that you didn't keep me posted on how she was doing. You may think it isn't any of my business but I *have* grown to care for her. It wasn't right."

Amy just stared at me for a while. She opened her mouth to say something but just then an employee walked into the barn, reeking of pot. She clutched a large grocery bag, filled with potato chips and Doritos, in her arms. Amy lifted her head and took a whiff of the scent, and belted out, "You're fired."

The girl swung around and glared at Amy. "You can't fire me. I am your brother's girlfriend."

"Let me say it more slowly, you.....are....fired. I wouldn't count on Mike standing by you because he hates drugs and druggies."

The girl dropped the bag of potato chips that she was fishing through. Julie lunged to grab a chip and the girl raised her arm as if to hit the dog. I have never seen anyone move as fast as Amy did as she soared across the room and grabbed the girl's arm. "I will break your arm over my knee if you touch my dog. Do you hear me?" She said this in a calm, measured voice, which made it scarier.

The girl nodded as Amy dragged the girl by her arm out of the building. When Amy re-entered the barn she strutted right to the phone. I watched her dial and say, "Hello? I am reporting a girl that is high as a kite driving down Barnum Road. She will take a right onto Clay Street soon. It is a red Honda Accord. Yes. Uh huh. Okay."

Amy looked indignant as she turned around. I held up my hands. "Hey, don't take it out on me. I'm not a dope fan either."

Amy looked around the barn and sighed. I asked her, "Do you want help with the stalls?"

She shook her head. "No. I like cleaning stalls when I have the time. I do my best thinking in the barn. Well, and when I'm asleep. Go figure."

After I was finished with the horses I tossed a ball for Julie for about 20 minutes. I could hear the other dogs complaining in the house.

"I gotta let them out to play, too. It's not fair." Amy stated as she walked toward the house.

The other dogs bolted out the door wagging their tails. They competed for the ball for a long while. My arm was getting tired. I couldn't believe the amount of energy the dogs expended, not tiring at all.

Exhausted, I headed to my next client. I realized that I was enjoying the time on the small farm on Barnum Road. When I first started working there the environment was tense and Amy unfriendly. Well, I wouldn't want to walk into her barn high or drunk, but I cannot really blame her for being mad about that.

* * *

Chapter 14

Amy's dog Linda was young. When it was time for her to go to the vet to be spayed, Amy called me to inquire about nice parks in my vicinity. "Why don't you just go home after you drop Linda off and go back to get her later?" The words, 'like a normal person' hung on my lips but, thankfully, I didn't utter them.

"My vet is an hour away, out by you. I don't want to be all the way in Geneva if something goes wrong. I thought Julie and I could just hike through a park to kill some time."

"You worry too much. What would go wrong?" I commented.

"You never know. But I am not going to sit in the vet's office all day with Julie. I don't like my dogs sitting around at the vet's. There are sick dogs in there."

I laughed. "That is some strange logic." I gave her directions to two different parks in the area.

Three days later, as I was gulping coffee and reading the newspaper, I spotted an interesting article. "Dog is Child's Best

Friend" it stated. I spit out some coffee as I sat straight up in my chair. There was a picture of Julie, with a little girl hugging her, in the paper.

> While picnicking in the park a 4 year old girl wandered away from her parents. Frantically searching for their child they were passed by a young woman clutching a leash, equally frantic, searching for her yellow lab who had escaped her collar. After the three made promises to look out for each others' lost wards, they all heard barking. The dog's owner took off in the direction of the barking. She soon discovered Julie, snuggled up next to a young girl, and licking the child's face.

> Amy Rowen, owner of the dog, Julie, took the two 'strays' on a walk to locate the little girl's parents. Having already notified the police of their daughters' disappearance, they were soon all joined by two police officers. The officers declined to give Rowen a citation for "dog at large" due to the circumstances.

> One of the policemen said, "That woman has one terrific dog! I don't know how she trained the dog to track like that. I wonder what her secret is."

I shook my head. Always an adventure with that dog. What a hero, I thought. I clipped the article from my newspaper so I could give it to Amy. This was definitely something for the scrapbook.

* * *

Chapter 15

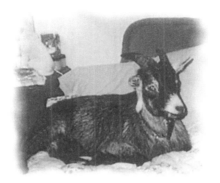

I had been the farm Farrier for years now. I had grown attached to all of the animals, horses and dogs. I had summers off because Amy would take all of her dogs and horses to her home in Canada for five months. I found myself missing them all. It was late September and I knew the whole group would be home the first week in October. Those last days went by slowly. I was ecstatic to get the call. After a long hard day with other clients the answering machine granted my wishes. "Hi. It's Amy. The horses are about due for new shoes when you get a chance."

It was still a whole week later before I could get out to Barnum Road. I practically ran into the barn, and started walking down the aisle way, saying hello to all my horse friends. I heard a strange noise, but ignored it, and continued greeting the horses. I felt something bang into the back of my legs. I turned around and looked down. It was a baby goat! He was adorable. Hearing the tack room door slide open, I looked up to see Amy grinning from ear to ear. "That's Petey. Isn't he great?"

I bent to pat the goat. He stood on his hind legs while I scratched him between the bumps on his head, soon to be horns. "Where did you get him?"

Amy looked sheepish. "We got him from a zoo in Orono, Ontario. It is illegal to move him across the border so I smuggled him." She said the last part with excitement; no remorse there.

She exited the tack room, Julie by her side, and played with Petey as we talked.

"You got him from a zoo?"

She nodded. "My niece and I went to the zoo one day and came home with a goat. My Mom was not pleased. First, we were late for dinner. Then when we arrive, we have a goat." Amy laughed. "She yelled, 'We can't trust you to go anywhere! Who goes to the ZOO and comes home with ANOTHER animal?'" Amy held her hands on her hips and mimicked her Mother.

It was then that I noticed Julie, standing about 30 feet away, looking sad. "C'mere Julie!" I called out. She tentatively wagged her tail but didn't move. Amy looked over her shoulder at the dog and explained. "She tried to eat Petey when she first met him. She got in BIG trouble. Now she is leery."

I walked over to Julie and sat on the floor with her. Soon she loosened up and rolled on the floor cheerfully. I gently batted her around for a while until Amy decided to return Petey to the house.

"The house?" I exclaimed.

"Sure. My Mom had him in the house in Canada. He cried when he was left outside. He is used to it. AND he is housebroken," Amy bragged. "Well, potty trained. He has a tendency to be a tad destructive in the house."

I laughed.

I continued to wrestle with Julie while Amy returned Petey to the house. As I watched her come back to the barn I noticed that she seemed more lighthearted than when she left for Canada.

We chatted while I trimmed the horse's feet. The phone rang and Amy ignored it. Julie started to get restless. "Aroooo," she cried. Amy looked her way but decided she was just upset about being in the tack room. The phone continued to ring. It rang three more times so she felt pressured to answer. Good thing she did because it was the alarm company telling her that they got a signal for a fire…in the house. Amy got off the phone and looked out a window. "I don't see smoke. We get false alarms all the time." She paused. "Maybe I better just run up there and check."

I heard some crashing so I put Lucy back in her stall and went to look out the door. The dogs were leaping out of a window and Petey followed. Smoke was pouring from the house window. Amy collected all of her animals for a moment, until the fire trucks arrived and the girls took off to chase them. Amy called them back with a harsh tone and they returned with their tails drooping, looking ashamed. I walked up to the house to see if I could help keep the dogs corralled for the time being. It didn't take long for the firemen to put out the fire that was contained to the kitchen. One of the men walked out with a partially charred roll of paper towel held outstretched in his hand. "It was mostly smoke, ma'am. However, the stovetop was turned on and there was a roll of paper towels strewn across the burners."

Amy slowly shifted her gaze to Petey. "Peeeeeteyyy?"

The fireman and I chuckled. Then the other man said, "I wouldn't be too hard on him. After all he pushed out the window and got the dogs out safely."

"Uh, I think it may have been the other way around. My dogs are very smart and…"

The fireman interrupted her. "No. I don't think so. There was a chair and then a small table pushed up to the counter beside the window. I've never seen a dog do that."

"Hmmm. You are probably right. Petey is always pushing stuff around with his head. Usually he is up to no good. We had to childproof *everything*."

"Not everything," the fireman corrected. "I suggest that you take the knobs off of the front of the oven. He probably was playing with it and accidently turned it on. Of course, goats have been known to live in a barn," he hinted.

* * *

Chapter 16

Julie kept winning ribbons after ribbons, after ribbons. Every trip to the farm there was a new bunch of ribbons that she had won at competitions. Amy and Julie seemed closer than ever. They were really working as a team. I was the Ferrier for Lake Farm Park during their Horse Fest. Amy and Julie were entered in the horse and hound competition. The horse and rider execute a small jumper's course, and then as they pass the finish line the dog and handler take off to do the agility course. Since I was mostly standing around all day, I hauled myself out to the competition field to watch. I am sure that Julie and Amy didn't start out this smooth. That day they looked like their event was choreographed. It looked like they were dancing. A few times I heard Amy yell out "right," or "left," and I'll be darned – Julie understood. Thankfully, the clock stops after the dog crosses the finish line because Amy was several yards behind Julie. I watched them collapse together on the lawn, Amy laughing and Julie "arrooooing."

They rolled around gleefully for a moment. An older woman walked past them and she glanced down. "Great run. I wish my dog could do agility. What's your secret?" she asked while passing. Amy just grinned at her dog as she pulled a pill bottle from her back pocket. After shaking a pill free she tossed it back and returned to rolling on the grass with her teammate. Then Julie spotted me. She charged over to me, ran circles around me and then jumped. There was something about Julie that made me feel special. I have watched her with others, especially children, and she seems to have the same effect on everyone. Julie makes you feel special. As if you were important to her, even if she has just met you... and that is part of what makes *her* so special.

Amy pulled herself up from the lawn and joined us. She tried to reach over and slip a noose around Julie's neck. Julie shot out away from her and halted in front of a woman. She stood and "Arf arf, arfed" in the woman's direction. I looked at Amy who was staring in awe at her dog in the distance. "What is she doing?"

Amy started to move forward toward her dog. "That is one of her alerts."

Confused, I followed Amy toward Julie. I had to pick up to a trot to keep up. "I thought she only alerted to you."

As Amy jogged beside me she said, "So did I. That is the norm. Dogs have to know your normal scent in order to determine when your scent changes. That's how she knows. But we don't know this woman."

We reached Julie and the startled woman. "Get your dog away from me. She is a bad dog, BAD dog." The woman raised her hand to Julie. Julie cowered and Amy jumped between them. A man clutching ice cream cones soon joined the rude woman. He held one out to the woman as they hurried away together, and he glanced over his shoulder at us with annoyance in his eyes. Amy caught up to the couple. "She was trying to tell you that your health is bad. I think. At least that is the way she tells me when I am sick."

I could see the woman snarl at Amy as she picked up her pace. The woman's escort took her arm as they marched away in a huff. Amy walked briskly back to Julie and me. "Why is that woman so angry? You'd think she would be grateful for the warning. What did she say?" I asked.

Amy rolled her eyes. "I should have left it alone. I don't even know for sure if she was alerting. After all, Julie just alerted to me five minutes ago. Maybe she was confused. The woman was pissed. 'Just because I'm fat, it doesn't mean I have health problems.'"

Amy shrugged it off, reached down, and wrapped the noose around Julie's neck. She patted her head and spoke to her. "You are a GOOD dog, a GREAT dog. Don't let the mean fat woman scare you." She said the last part in baby talk. Julie gazed into her mother's eyes and thumped her tail tentatively.

Amy and Julie returned to the competition site. As they left, Amy said, "We have to go pick up our ribbon."

I called after her, "How do you know you won a ribbon?"

Amy just looked over her shoulder and smiled, and then she glanced down at her dog.

I returned to my post in the barn. I leaned against the door jam and watched the various activities outside. I heard the ambulance before I saw it. I stood straight and stared at it as it passed. I had to know. I walked briskly through the barn area and followed the ambulance with my eyes. It stopped at the sheep barn and I quickened my pace to catch up. I could soon see the woman that Amy and Julie had irritated being hoisted onto a stretcher. I kept my distance so I would not cause a commotion. I was certain that the man accompanying the woman had seen me with Amy and Julie. Didn't seem like a good time to anger him further. As I was watching the paramedics work, out of the corner of my eye I saw something moving toward me at a fast rate. I turned my head, prepared to ward off a Bull or an Ostrich, and spotted the woman's companion. He was out of breath as he reached toward me. I jumped back. He kept his hand outstretched as he said, "Thank you so much for what you and your friend did. My wife felt pain in her left arm and felt nauseated. If it weren't for the two of you we would have dismissed it as fatigue or something, indigestion maybe. I called the ambulance and by the time they got here she had collapsed. You two are very nice indeed." He finally let go of my hand and I reciprocated.

"Actually it was the dog that knew something was wrong, not us."

The man looked surprised. "Well, that is some dog! Isn't that amazing that a dog could do such a thing? What is her secret?"

I just shook my head slowly and smiled. As the paramedics hustled to close the back door of the ambulance, the man trotted toward them, waving his arms. "Wait. I have to go with her." Soon the vehicle drove past me and I turned to watch.

Having returned to my post, I once again was bored watching the festivities. I saw Amy driving by in her SUV. Julie had her nose pressed against the window. When Amy spotted me she held up a blue ribbon and waved it toward me. I pretended to applaud while chuckling and shaking my head. She sure had gotten cocky!

I could hardly wait to tell Amy that Julie was right, once again.

* * *

Chapter 17

The Pony, Bill, was by far the hardest to manage when I had to trim his feet. He had come from a very abusive environment and had developed strong defensive skills. I would usually have Kris or Amy hold him in the arena while I worked. There was less for Bill to run into in the arena, which decreased the odds of him getting hurt. Of course it increased the odds that I might get hurt since the Pony had more room to move.

Truth be told, Bill the Pony cracked me up. He had become an escape artist, much to Mike's dismay. Bill never left the property but he was known to hold up the occasional UPS truck. He and Petey the goat often played mischievous games with visitors. On more than one occasion I saw a farm hand being dragged around by the Pony. Bill had an appetite, though, so usually one shake of the treat jar brought him running.

Earlier in the day, while I was working on Milton's feet, I heard a crashing sound. Milton jumped and I had to investigate. Petey had pushed a treat jar off a shelf and was nudging it toward

Bill's stall. I watched with amusement while Milton got control of his nerves. Petey stood on the jar while Bill, head ducked under his stall door, worked on unscrewing the lid. It would have worked, too, if I hadn't intervened. The lid was halfway off by the time I decided that enough was enough. Of course I did take a treat out of the jar for each of them. I am a believer that ingenuity should be rewarded, not stifled.

There had been workmen on the farm all day doing repairs here and there. They seemed annoyed that they were asked not to work on the barn roof while I was there. Banging overhead is never conducive to shoeing horses; I don't care how calm the horse normally is. So I was quite annoyed when I was struggling to manage Bill in the horse arena and I could hear commotion overhead. As the Pony swung his rear away from me I stood up and told Amy, "I cannot do this if those guys are going to be on the roof."

Amy nodded. "I don't see what their problem is. I told them that as long as you are here they couldn't work on this roof. It isn't as if there is a lack of other work to be done." She handed me Bill's lead line and turned to exit the arena. Julie was always relegated to the tack room when a horse was out in the barn area. There were no such rules for Petey. Petey followed Amy as she exited the barn. He would run to catch up to her, then head butt her in the rear playfully. I was still listening to light tapping on the roof when a commotion arose from outside of the barn. I concentrated my efforts on calming Bill until I heard a yelp escape Amy. I released Bill into the arena, hoping that he would run off a little of his nervous energy, pulled a board across the entrance, and hightailed it outside. Amy was climbing a ladder that was leaning against the barn. There were two men pacing twenty feet away, each nervously puffing on a cigarette. A third man was steadily holding a ladder. "What's going on?" I asked. No sooner had the words left my mouth when I saw Julie trotting the length of the barn roof.

"Oh my God!" I said with alarm. I started to climb the ladder but Amy yelled down to me. "Stay put."

"How are you going to get her down?" I asked.

"Carefully!" She snapped.

I realized I was holding my breath when I spotted part of the problem. There was a squirrel on top of the roof. Julie seemed determined to catch the squirrel. The squirrel, equally determined, was trying to find a way off the roof. There weren't any trees close enough to the barn that would allow the squirrel to make his escape. So, a chase ensued. The two men in the background were equally distracted because Petey took the opportunity to gently pull a pack of cigarettes from one of their pockets. I started to say something when out of the corner of my eye I saw the ladder shudder and I returned my gaze to Amy. Amy was climbing off the ladder onto the roof; she lumbered without grace, practically falling flat on her stomach. As Amy was starting to right herself Julie raced by her, tongue hanging out of the side of her grinning mouth. Amy made a grab for the dog but Julie tucked her butt under just in time to avoid her Mother's reach.

Amy stood on the roof and called to her dog in a surprisingly calm voice. "Julie, come."

Julie walked toward her mother but hesitated about five feet away, again just out of reach. Amy bent at the waist and patted her legs. "Come."

This time, head hanging low, Julie complied. Amy held onto the scruff around Julie's collarless neck as she walked the dog slowly to the edge of the barn where the ladder was. She looked over the edge. "Yep. I'm gonna need some help up here."

I looked over my shoulder. The two men that were pacing earlier were now searching their pockets and the surrounding ground for the missing pack of cigarettes. I shrugged and headed up the ladder. As I climbed onto the roof I asked, "Now what?"

"I'm going to get in position on the ladder. I need YOU to back Julie up to me and I am going to walk her backwards down the ladder. Don't let go of her until I have ahold of her though."

"Well, duh." I said as I watched Julie's gaze drift toward an out-of-breath squirrel. The squirrel sat perched on the peak of the roof as if watching the scene unfold. I used my hand to move Julie's head so she could not stare at the squirrel. I figured, out of sight, out of mind.

Amy was on the ladder and I backed Julie up so that her butt was practically in her mother's face. Amy used her right arm to pull Julie's back right foot off the roof and onto a rung on the ladder. She held Julie with her left arm under the dogs hips. Amy started to back down and I could see the panic in the dog's eyes. Julie tried to struggle away from her Mother's grasp, Amy wobbled a tad, and held on. I called down to the men below. "You guys all get on this ladder and hold it steady. If they start to fall you catch them," I demanded.

Amy rolled her eyes up at me. She looked nervous as she alternated her arms, one placing a hind foot on a lower ladder rung, the other clasped around her dog's waist. Again, I saw fear in Julie's eyes. "This ought to teach her a lesson," I said.

Amy didn't comment. Slowly they descended the ladder. I heard a chipper sound behind me. The squirrel had moved closer to the edge of the barn. As soon as Amy had Julie's feet firmly on the ground I let out a sigh of relief. My relief was premature because Julie spotted the squirrel, gazing over the side of the roof, and she started up the ladder again. I waved my arms furiously and yelled "NO" in a firm tone. Julie looked at me with confusion in her eyes but she jumped two feet down and off the ladder.

Amy stood shaking her head, "Are you KIDDING ME, Julie?"

Julie hung her head and lay down. Amy glared at the dog. Julie rolled on her back while maintaining eye contact with Amy. Amy scowled. Julie thumped her tail. Amy smiled. Julie rolled over and ran to her Mother's side. Amy scratched Julie's rump as I made my climb down from the roof. Both feet planted on the ground I turned to the guys holding the ladder. "Get that thing down on the ground until you need it." They nodded and struggled with the ladder until it was laid flat on the ground.

I walked over to Julie and looked down at her, hands on my hips. She smiled and thumped her tail some more. I reached down and scratched her behind her ears. Shaking my head I said to Amy, "Can't believe that just happened."

Petey was lying in the gazebo, still munching on cigarettes. I watched as the three men walked toward the dog gym, one of them still searching through his back pockets for the missing smokes.

I entered the barn and saw that Amy had Julie in a "time-out" in the tack room. The door to the room was closed. She slid the door closed behind her as she exited and let out a long sigh of relief. Hands on hips she said, "THAT'S the kind of stuff I'm talking about."

I chuckled. "Has she done that before?"

"NO!" She exclaimed. "That's part of the trouble, she thinks up these inventive ways to torture me. Things no normal person would anticipate."

A whimper sounded from the other side of the door and Amy slid the door slowly open. Julie pushed her head through the small opening. Her head hung low, she raised her eyes toward Amy and raised her eyebrows.

"Hmmm, hmmmm. Do you feel any shame?" Amy asked.

Julie lunged through the door, wagging her tail and jumped up on Amy and began licking her face.

"That's a no," I said.

Amy gently pushed Julie off her and scratched her behind her ears. "Can you even imagine how cool that was FOR HER?"

We were all startled by the sound of a crash. Amy pointed at the tack room and said firmly to Julie, "Go." Julie trotted into the tack room and laid down, head between her front paws.

I was only a few feet ahead of Amy when she rounded the corner from the barn to the attached arena. "Crap," I said as I saw the open door to the living room that runs off the arena. Bill was in the living room, head in the refrigerator, pulling out packages of cookies.

Amy stopped in the doorway as I grabbed Bill's halter and pulled him away from the scattered cookies. I used my foot to push the refrigerator door open. I had to turn Bill in a tight circle to lead him back to the arena. Amy was standing in the doorway, hands on hips.

I could feel myself blush. "I'm sorry. I swear I pulled the board across the arena entrance." I pointed to the board that was still in place.

Amy smiled. "There are two boards we use for Bill." She pointed to a lower board and brackets. "He can get over one and under the other."

I shook my head as I reached out to move the upper board. Bill broke free from my grip and ducked under the board. He ran in happy circles, kicking up his heels for a few minutes. I was pulling the lower board across the arena entrance when I heard the familiar "baaaaing" of Petey. The small goat trotted into the area that attached the barn to the arena. He spotted the open door to the living room and his face lit up. He charged in and I could hear Amy say firmly, "Don't even THINK about it." The little guy was not deterred and as I joined Amy in the task of cleaning up the mess of strewn cookies, it was a race for Petey to see how much he could eat before we got the cookies off of the floor. At one point we were laughing as we grabbed for cookie carnage before Petey could snatch it up. Amy, holding onto the bottom of her shirt, had made a small pouch where she was holding cookies. As I stood up, dusting cookie crumbs from my knees, I spotted Petey opening the refrigerator. "No," I exclaimed as I lunged forward to shut the refrigerator door. Petey looked at me; cheeks filled with cookies, then turned and ran out of the living room.

I helped Amy up from the floor. "I cannot believe he can open the refrigerator!"

Amy started to transfer the cookies into a garbage can. Dusting off her shirt she replied, "How do you think Bill got into it?"

I shrugged. "Petey was outside with us, though."

She shook her head. "Not the whole time. He's a fast little bugger when he's up to no good. That is why all the drawers and cupboards are childproofed in the house. I've had to bungee cord tables and chairs so he can't push them around with his head, and the trash is hung high, like bear bags when you go camping."

"Sounds like a pain in the ass. Ever consider putting him in the barn?" I asked.

"Nope, he wouldn't be happy. He is housebroken and he is playful and funny. He adds too much to life in the house."

By now Bill was watching us through the large window that overlooks the arena. His nostrils flared as he expelled his breath. I moaned. "He doesn't look calm."

Amy laughed, "Sugar high." She pressed her hand against the window where Bill's muzzle pushed against the other side. "Well, let's go, cowboy. We still have to get his feet trimmed."

I moaned some more as I reluctantly followed Amy out to the arena. "Nothing's ever easy here," I complained. "It's always something...."

* * *

Chapter 18

There were so many years that I was allowed to share in the accomplishments, altruism and even companionship of Julie. But I hadn't seen Julie, or Amy for that matter, in a very long time.

Kris filled me in while she held the horses for me. "Amy's Mother died at home. This was a huge shock to everyone. Her Mom was in great health. The funeral was a little over a month ago. I'm surprised you didn't know."

I shook my head. "I feel horrible. I would've gone to the calling hours. Where is she now?"

Kris looked at me with a mischievous grin. "That's hard to say. I think I believe in heaven. It may not be all sunshine and lollipops but…"

I interrupted "Amy, not her Mother! Smart ass."

Kris' expression turned grim as she fed Prince a carrot and answered, "At the vet with Petey. He is really sick."

I placed Prince's foot on the ground and stood up. As I turned to Kris I said, "Oh no! Petey is her baby. I can't think of anything worse right now." I wiped my brow with the back of my hand.

"Well, that vet that told Amy to feed Petey grain is an idiot. She shouldn't be a vet because she didn't know that goats, especially neutered males, should not eat grain. Petey got sick three years ago and had surgery at the Ohio State veterinary hospital. He had another surgery two days after Amy's Mother died. It's been touch and go since then."

We both perked up as we heard a car pull down the drive. Kris leaned so she could see the driveway, "It's Amy."

"God, I hope she has Petey with her."

Kris and I watched as Amy slid out of the truck, and Julie hopped out behind her. She went to the back of the truck, where Petey's pillow stayed. She lifted the 80 pound boy down, gently placing him on the ground. Petey did not look like himself. His head held low; his steps cautious. This was not the little mischief maker I knew.

Petey spotted us in the doorway and slowly started on a path to greet us. Amy and Julie followed at a slow pace. When he was in reach I took a few steps forward to pat the small goat. He rubbed against me. I looked up to see Amy and Julie approaching. "So what is the story?"

Her eyes filled with tears but she choked them back quickly. "There is nothing else that can be done. If he keeps peeing he should be fine. His bladder is torn, though, so if the urine leaks into his body we're done."

"He's awfully tired," I observed.

Amy nodded, "We had a long night and then a long day at the vet."

Julie tentatively approached Petey. She "Arroooo'ed." We all looked at each other. Amy looked defeated. "Shit," she said.

"Maybe she is wrong." Kris offered.

Amy and I exchanged knowing glances.

"Maybe I should take him up to the house so he can get some rest." Amy patted her leg and called Petey. "C'mon Petey," she coaxed. He very slowly turned to follow her. Kris and I watched their slow progression toward the house. Amy and Julie obviously reached the house first. They turned to wait for Petey. I watched Amy sit down Indian-style in her driveway. Julie snuggled next to her. Petey staggered a little and then, when he reached Amy, he crawled in her lap and collapsed. We witnessed Amy break down as she laid her head on the goat and sobbed.

Catching her breath she leaned to the right to retrieve her cell phone from her back pocket. As we watched Amy on the phone I turned to look at Kris. Tears trailing down her cheeks, she sobbed, "Oh God, that's the call."

I looked confused. "What call?"

Kris rolled her eyes at me, "To the vet."

Still not catching on, "I thought the vet couldn't do any more for him?"

As Kris turned away from me she said, "There's just one thing left that they can do."

I watched her pull a horse cooler from a rod and THEN I caught on. "Oh God. Oh No!"

As Kris passed me, carrying the cooler, she said, "Look at him. She won't let him suffer."

I stood frozen in the doorway. I heard Prince pawing in the wash stall impatiently. I called to him, "Hold on." I stared after Kris who carried the cooler to Amy and covered Petey with it. I saw them exchange some words before Kris retreated.

I returned to Prince and finished replacing his last shoe. As I walked him to his stall Kris walked through the barn briskly and straight to the tack room where she slammed the door. I could hear soft sobbing through the closed door while I swept the wash stall floor.

A car was slowing in the driveway as I was packing up my truck. My heart skipped a beat, thinking it was the vet. A woman and a young girl dashed out of the car and to Amy's side. They sat in a small circle around Petey and cried. Julie started to pace and pant. She was obviously stressed out by the grief. Her head snapped my way and she ran to my side. I patted her head and spoke to her softly, "I'm not sure if you should be here. Your Mom might need you." Her ears perked up and she looked over her shoulder at Amy clutching Petey. She turned and sauntered back toward the house.

A van started down the drive and Julie playfully started to chase it. Amy didn't call her off. I then realized why. Amy didn't what to yell over Petey. I took charge and commanded Julie to 'Come.' She trotted to me with a disappointed look on her face. I held her back while the van passed. The driver looked grim. Emily. I didn't want to be around for this. I walked Julie up to Amy, then hightailed it back to my truck. As soon as I finished packing up my belongings I hopped in the driver's seat. I put the truck in gear, but before I could pull away I heard Julie howling. Amy soon joined her. Amy was not joking around. The two raised their heads and wailed toward the sky. I abruptly stepped on the accelerator and my truck lurched forward. It was too much. The gate was mercifully open so I could drive straight through. Just as I believed I had made my escape I noticed the stream of involuntary tears on my face.

* *

Petey's Memorial Service was October 11, 2009.

* * *

Chapter 19

When I arrived six weeks later I saw the same ominous van parked in the barn drive. I pulled over to the side of the drive and walked to the barn. There was a great deal of activity in the barn. Everybody was fussing over the Pony, Bill; he had soaked towels hanging off him. Emily was holding an IV bag in the air. Amy was pacing; Julie shadowed every step. Amy looked at Julie and seemed startled. "Hey, back in the room. Go," she commanded as she pointed toward the tack room.

I stopped Amy and asked, "Should I wait to get a horse out of their stall?"

She nodded. Emily's bag had been drained. She unclipped the bag from the catheter, taped the catheter to Bill's side and walked out of the stall. As she tossed the empty bag in the garbage she sighed, "I think we have to get him out of here. He has been on antibiotics for three days and his temperature is still elevated. "

What is it now?" Amy inquired.

"104.3. We need to get him into a hospital," Emily explained.

Amy nodded and walked toward the door. Feeling helpless yet again, I called after her, "Do you want help hooking up the trailer?"

She continued walking and yelled over her shoulder, "I've had it hooked up for two days."

I retreated further into the barn and sat on a chair in the corner. I could hear Emily on the phone. I listened as she made the referral to the hospital. "I don't know if he's gonna make it. We've had him on heavy antibiotics for three days and his temperature just keeps skyrocketing'" She glanced at me and noticed I was eavesdropping. She frowned and took the phone outside.

I saw Kris gathering freshly soaked towels for Bill. I walked over to Bill's stall and watched her replace the old with the new. "God, it's always something around here isn't it? How does Amy handle it?"

Kris looked at me. "Welcome to her life."

Emily moved her van and I could hear Amy's truck and trailer getting close. I went outside to guide her back but she never looked at me. She hopped out of the truck and started lowering the back ramp of the trailer. I helped and said, "Guess you've done this before, huh?" She flashed a glare at me and moved to the barn.

Soon Bill was led onto the trailer, his legs were wrapped, and he had a catheter in his neck. His head was drooped and he moved slowly. Not a good sign, I thought to myself. I got out of the way and watched Amy haul the trailer down the drive. I again felt helpless. I pulled Hammlet out of his stall and took him down the aisle. I could still hear the roar of the truck's engine in the distance.

I got the call on April 23 at 11:23 p.m. "This is just a courtesy call. I am heading to the hospital."

I must really be dense because my reply was, "For what?"

I could hear the irritation in Amy's voice, "He is slowly, painfully, dying. I have to let him go."

"Where's he gonna go?"

"I have no idea. Probably to heaven since he is a Pony. I think all animals go to heaven because they are pure of heart and they never sin. I mean, animals only kill for survival, food, protection; and people, well...."

I had to interrupt. "Oh my God, You mean you're going to put him down?"

I must have been on speakerphone because I could hear Kris in the background. "Ding, ding, ding, ding. You won a prize. Johnny, tell Ron what he has won."

* *

Bill's Memorial Service was March 2, 2010.

* * *

Chapter 20

It had only been two weeks since Bill's Memorial service. I was deeply hoping that today would be uneventful. I got my wish. There was a pot of coffee brewing in what Amy called the living room. Who has a living room in their barn? She also had a gas fireplace on. The aroma of fresh flowers lingered in the air. There actually were fresh flowers in April's hayrack and in Bill's stall. The music of *Lehey,* a Canadian singing group from the same town in Canada where Amy lived during the summer, was playing. Lakefield, I think.

A heavyset woman I had never met came hobbling in the barn at the same time that Amy and Hammlet appeared from the horse arena. I looked around. "Where is Julie?"

"In the living room, why?"

"I didn't see her in there. I was just wondering."

Amy handed me Hammy's reins and turned a corner to the living room. "Julie?" I heard her call quietly. Then the two of them came around the corner. "She was in her crate."

Julie spotted Hammlet and retreated to the living room, pouting.

Just then I felt a shadow hanging over me. The big woman was closing in. "I am Pam Martin." She held out her hand. "I work here now," she stated proudly.

I looked over at Amy, "What happened to Kris?"

"She is still around but we needed some extra help. Right now she's meeting a new client at the Pet Food Bank."

I must have looked puzzled because Amy explained further. "The Foundation is starting to take more of my time. When I have time to be in the barn I'd rather ride the horses, and I had to fire Karen that day she showed up trashed."

"I know all about horses. I used to work at Lake Erie College," Pam offered excitedly.

Amy brushed Hammlet after taking his tack off. She looked over at me. "Why don't you just start with him so I can go take the dogs to the gym? Pam can hold the horses for you."

I figured she, once again, didn't want to hang out in the barn. Even I got a knot in my stomach when I passed Bill's stall.

Amy left, Julie racing to catch up, tossing a suspicious look at Pam as she passed.

Pam talked nonstop while I was trimming the horse's feet. "I really like my job. I get to do what I love and get paid for it. It's great. I love animals. I think Amy is great, don't you? I mean she takes such good care of her animals. When I came for the interview we met in her kitchen because she was making her own dog food for all of those dogs."

I stopped her. "Hey Pam, why don't you start cleaning stalls or something? Prince is the last horse I have to shoe and they will all go outside after I am done."

"The horses are in their stalls."

I grimaced. "Prince isn't. Clean his stall," I suggested.

Pam looked confused. "Oh, okay. I guess I can do that." Instead I watched her organize the pitchforks and shovels. She wiped some shelves off with a damp rag. She seemed to have mastered the skill of procrastination. This was not a motivated woman.

Kris entered the barn as I was putting Prince out to the side pasture. "He still looks sad," she said as she watched Prince saunter out to where there was a hay barrel.

I nodded, "Sure. He was always out with Bill. They were buddies."

Pam came looming over us. Kris looked annoyed. "Why don't you start cleaning stalls?"

Pam was disappointed. "Oh. Okay."

Kris and I exchanged a look of doubt. I whispered, "She thinks she knows everything but she does nothing."

Kris smiled and nodded. She then turned and started putting the thoroughbreds out in their pasture. As she led Lucy by Pam she reminded her, "Remember, you get paid for the work you DO, not the time you spend here."

Pam went into the tack room and rifled through a brown paper bag. She came up with a donut that she stuffed in her mouth. Mystery solved, I thought.

I was cleaning the wash stall when I heard Kris return, carrying two horses leads. She slapped them on a counter and turned to Pam, who was still eating donuts. "Pam, you need to get your work done. The horses come in at sundown. Their stalls need to be ready."

Pam, with her mouth full of donuts and sugar all over her face, nodded vigorously. "I just want to run up to the dog gym and put my clothes in the wash. Amy said it was okay as long as I use my own laundry detergent."

Kris rolled her eyes. "Fine, but you have to get back down to the barn in a hurry to get started on chores."

Pam nodded as she got her instructions.

With a sigh Kris added, "I'll get started on the stalls."

Pam lumbered out of the barn in a hurry.

I leaned on the tack room door. "Want some help? I feel partially responsible because I was a little late. The horses didn't get out early enough."

"No. Thanks for the offer, though."

We chatted for a while until Amy came pounding into the barn. Julie was behind her but had paused to jump at a butterfly. "Uh oh. Something is amiss." Kris muttered.

Amy stormed into the room. "Do you want to tell me why fat Pam is sitting in the dog grooming area, NAKED?"

Kris burst out in laughter. "What?"

I stepped back and snickered to myself.

"You heard me!" she yelled just as Julie caught up to her. She lowered her voice. "Julie and I were in the gym. When we were done we walked through the grooming area. What did I see? Not only is she fat, with rolls and rolls, but her chest was covered with chocolate sprinkles and there were drips of jelly on her too."

I lowered my voice and added, "Well, she DOES like donuts."

Kris was laughing hard now. "She...she said you gave her permission to wash her clothes here."

"NOT THE ONES SHE HAS ON!" Amy exclaimed.

At this we all broke into uncontrollable laughter. We were still chortling when Pam lumbered into the barn, holding a towel around her large frame. We all looked over at her and burst into huge guffaws. Amy was practically choking as she uttered, "Pam, you... you are fired."

After we watched Pam's vehicle putter down the driveway we all took deep breaths. I shook my head. "Wow. That was one for the record books. When I called you about changing my appointment I thought you said you had hired a crotchety old guy named Norman."

Amy was leaning against the wall. "Yeahhhhh. Well, he didn't work out either."

I snorted. "Why? I HAVE to ask."

Julie came up behind Kris. When the dog's head was even with Kris' hip the woman dropped her hand and gently stroked Julie's head. Then Kris rolled her eyes. "Norman called in sick."

"That sounds reasonable," I put in my two cents. "Ever think you are too used to firing people?"

Amy stood and shook her head. "He wouldn't come to work because he had gas."

I nodded, "Wow! That must have been some gas! Maybe he did you a favour by staying home."

Kris chimed in, "He had gas for *three* days."

Again, I said, "Wow." I glanced at Julie and she stared back.

"What are you doing?" Amy asked.

"I was just noticing Julie looks different. I can't put my finger on why…" my voice trailed off.

Kris started chuckling as Amy explained, "She has contact lenses."

"What? For dogs?" I was in disbelief.

Amy nodded, "Yep. It wasn't easy to find but the Ophthalmologist at State Veterinary Specialties really outdid herself." Amy kneeled beside Julie. Julie turned her head so she could lick Amy's face.

I snapped my fingers to get Julie's attention. I bent down and looked closely at her eyes. "I'll be damned. Now I've seen everything. What was wrong with her eyes?"

Amy turned her head and planted a kiss right under Julie's nose, then struggled to stand. "Not much. She sees pretty well under normal circumstances, but when she was running flyball she was pulling away from the jumps. I had her checked out by Dr. Eldridge at my regular Animal Clinic and she checked out fine. Then it occurred to me that she might have trouble seeing the jumps. They are all white in color. She obviously had the energy and desire to continue with the sport; otherwise, I wouldn't have bothered. But anyway, she just has to wear them on and off for a while to get her eyes used to them."

"Geesh. How often do you go to the vet?"

110

Amy smiled. "I shoulda been invited to my vet's kid's graduation from college."

I shook my head. "You should have married a vet....for YOUR money."

Amy shrugged. "I'm not too much of an alarmist but I don't hesitate to go to the vet if there could be something wrong. Nip it in the bud, so to speak."

Kris stepped up. "She just goes as often as she needs to. I met them once, very nice."

Amy added, "They have been my vets for 27 years. They have NEVER made a mistake with my dogs. In 27 years. *Never.*"

As she was leaving the barn with Julie trailing behind I asked Kris, "What is flyball?"

"It's a dog team sport. It's a relay race. Dogs jump over four jumps; the height depends on what size the smallest dog on the team is, and they turn on a big box that spits out a tennis ball. The dogs grab the tennis ball and run back over the jumps, passing their teammate on the same line. It's harder to master than it looks."

I rubbed my forehead with the back of my hand. "So Julie is on a team. What team?"

"Amy started her own team. Her Border Collie Cinder was the first dog to be drawn to it. She was on another team but the other people took things too seriously. Amy said it felt like team practice was something she was doing TO her dog, instead of with her."

"What's the team name?" I really didn't know why I was asking all of these questions. I had no idea what the game was about.

"Spoiled Sports."

"Huh. Why?" Again with the questions.

Kris grinned. "Because when our dogs stop having fun we take our balls and go home."

Spoiled Sports

I chuckled. "Well, I think we should all have that philosophy about everything, if ya think about it."

I shook my head slowly as I was walking toward my truck. "So Julie has contacts now. I'll be a monkey's uncle."

* * *

Chapter 21

I spotted an ad in the paper. It read, "Part time help wanted. Hard work for so-so pay, strict boss, must have REAL experience with REAL horses and dogs, have your own transportation, be drug free, no criminal records or tendencies, and never be naked at work." The Barnum Road address was listed.

I chortled. "That ad sure has gotten long," I said aloud to myself. Every time an employee or candidate has a serious, unemployable flaw, it is added to the new "Help Wanted" ad.

I pulled myself out of my Lazyboy chair, grabbed my empty coffee mug and headed to the kitchen. I was running water in the coffee cup when the phone rang. I checked the caller ID. Ugh, my ex-wife.

I answered the phone anyway. She rattled on for a few seconds before I fully understood what she was telling me. She took our, well hers now, dog to the vet. When she opened the driver's side door to get in, Poochy leapt out and took off running into a thick wooded area. She can't find her anywhere.

I phoned Amy to explain why I was going to be late. She offered to haul Julie out to Bainbridge to help us look for Poochy. I eagerly accepted her offer.

We all met at the vet's office. When Amy got out of her truck with Julie my ex, Sherri, snapped, "Who is this, your girlfriend?"

Amy overheard, and as she and Julie got closer she answered, "Not even close. Now do you want help finding your dog or not?"

Sherri blushed and nodded. "Sorry. Thanks for helping." She handed me a picture of Poochy who was a black and white Labradoodle. Amy handed the picture back to Sherri. "I am hoping there is only one lost dog out there. I won't need the photo."

We all entered the wooded area together; then Amy stopped. "There are four of us. Why don't you two each take a different direction? I'll go this way until she gets a scent." Amy released a long lead so that Julie could work ahead of her. I watched Julie pull Amy off in a direction; an extra leash was hanging out of Amy's back pocket. I smiled. "Cocky."

It had been two discouraging hours and I was spent. As I was trying to find my way back to my car my cell phone rang. "We've got Poochy," Amy sang. "Meet me back at the cars."

I was so relieved. Poochy would not do well as a stray. I reached the cars first. It took me a moment to notice Sherri's car was gone. I called her on her cell phone. When she answered I could hear sounds of a restaurant in the background. "Where are you?"

"I'm at Starbucks. Since that woman has a tracking dog I figured I couldn't compete with that so I went after some hot coffee."

I hung up without another word. "What a bitch," I said aloud.

It wasn't much longer before Amy, Julie, and Poochy came bursting through the woods across the street. As Amy was tugged across the street by the two dogs she looked around. When she reached me she asked, "Where's your ex-wife?"

I explained and Amy's response was, "What a bitch."

I shrugged. "I am sorry. She is never very appreciative."

Amy said. "That's okay. I came out here for Poochy. Not you or your ex. By the way, I have to ask you a question…"

I smiled. "Sherri named her."

Amy nodded. "Ohhhh. That makes more sense." She handed Poochy's lead to me and fussed over Julie as they returned to her SUV.

"I'll be at the farm as soon as I can," I yelled after them.

Amy held her hand in the air and waved. I looked down at Poochy and smiled. "Good to see ya, girl." I looked at the leash again. Maybe Amy isn't so cocky. She just knows her dog.

* * *

Chapter 22

It was July 23, 2010. A beautiful sunny day. Kris met me when I got into the Barnum Road barn. "Hey. Amy took the girls to a vet appointment today."

"Is somebody sick?" I asked.

Kris said happily, "Nope, just a well-baby checkup. All is well."

We chatted happily while she held Lucy and Milton. "Since the other two are easy can I get up to the house to bake horse cookies?"

"Sure," I answered.

"You're sure you don't mind?"

"Nope What is on the horse's TV today? Maybe I could just turn it up."

"They're watching *'Dreamer'*" she giggled.

"Again?" I complained.

"Again! Its Lucy's favorite," she said as she grabbed her water bottle and headed out.

I had a nice serene afternoon with the horses. They were relaxed and quiet. I was just finishing Hammlet's feet when Kris came back to the barn. I looked up. "Hey stranger. Got those horse treats in the oven?"

She didn't answer. I glanced at her again and noticed that she looked ashen. I placed Hammy's foot on the mat and stood up. "What's wrong?"

She burst into tears. "Julie has cancer."

I gasped, "What? How? I have never seen a healthier dog in my life. Amy takes GREAT care of her, well all of her animals, but especially Julie. I don't understand."

"She has to have surgery Monday. They will try to remove the tumor, but..." she was crying heavily now.

As I pulled away from the barn I spotted Amy on the children's swing absently tossing a ball for Julie. Amy was just staring into space.

I sent Amy a consoling email late that night. I got a reply Monday night. From what Kris had told me Julie was to have surgery that day.

> Friends,
>
> I was stunned to learn of a tumor that was found during a simple annual physical. After all five girls had been examined, Dr. Jim said, "Let's go play with the ultra sound machine." Immediately I was suspicious.....duh. He spotted a tumor next to Julie's bladder, just above a main artery. The concern is great enough that I waited while he re-scheduled two surgeries set for Monday to get her

in immediately. This was not even on my radar; there were no clinical symptoms AT ALL.

We had a long day (8 a.m. - 5:30p.m..... I was the "Wal-Mart" greeter for the vet's office). Julie's X-rays showed some fluid in her lungs. There is also a shadow on her lungs. The biopsy in her abdomen could not be taken laproscopically due to the location of the tumor - too close to the femoral artery..... so, she had to be opened up. Odds are the tumor is secondary and malignant but I'll wait for biopsy results before I borrow that trouble.

Probably what will happen next is we will get a better look at the lungs via CT scan or MRI. Everyone responds differently to chemo and radiation so I am approaching this timidly and I have to consider quality vs. quantity of time.

I'll keep you posted,

Amy (Julie's Mom)

Two days later I got another email from Amy.

July 28

The biopsy results are back. Julie has a histiocytic sarcoma which is an aggressive cancer in connective tissues i.e.: tendons, muscles, even blood. Chemotherapy is usually unsuccessful and the prognosis is poor. I was told that dogs do not usually have more than 3 months to live with this cancer.

We are going to Metropolitan Veterinary Hospital tomorrow and have an appointment at Ohio State August 1.

Julie's Mom

When a third email arrived August 13th I hesitated in opening it. However it read,

118

Julie and I were at an agility trial this weekend. She got two first place ribbons, and more importantly, she felt good and was happy!

Julie's Mom

* * *

Chapter 23

It was mid-September now, and I couldn't find words to express how relieved and excited I was to watch Julie run towards my truck as I poked my way down the driveway. Instead of yelling at her to get back from the truck, I opened my truck door so she could leap in. She sat on my lap until we reached the barn.

Amy walked outside from the barn and spotted Julie in my lap. She laughed, and when I opened the passenger side door Amy called out to Julie. Julie ran to her mother's side and spun in circles in front of her.

I hauled myself out of my truck, a big grin on my face. Julie ran back and forth between us. I looked at Amy, "She looks great! How sure are they that the tumor was cancer?"

The smile waned. "100%. She gets radiation every three weeks and I give her oral chemo twice a day. I have her on an herbal supplement too. "

I shook my head. "She seems like herself, though." I looked Amy in the eye. "You're going to get more than three months."

"I hope so," she said as she headed into the barn.

Julie and I followed. I decided to drop the subject and allow Amy to just enjoy every happy moment she has with Julie.

"We had an agility trial last week and she cleaned up! She ran like a champ! We had so much fun. Linda and Jill both ran well, too. Linda got a title and Jill got a first and a second in her events."

"We go back to Columbus tomorrow," she said sadly.

"Where do you stay?" I asked.

She lifted her head. "We stay at the Sheraton. We swim in the pool for a while and order room service. The rooms are huge so sometimes we play hide and seek."

"Okay. I have to ask. Do you swim naked in the pool at the Sheraton?"

"NO! Are you crazy?" She scolded.

I shrugged. "Well, it seems you are always swimming naked HERE."

"Not in public. Besides, why wouldn't I swim naked with my dog?"

I shrugged again. "Guess you're not shy, is all."

"Shy? My relationship with Julie is unconditional, and non-judgmental. Do you think that she cares if I'm naked? Really, when I think about it, I have much closer relationships with my dogs than I have ever had with a human."

I had to change the subject. "Tell me more about hide'n'seek. How do you do that?"

"Watch," she said. She put Julie in a stay. A few seconds later we both heard her call, "Julie, come."

I followed the dog. As soon as she got into the horse arena she put her nose to the ground. She walked a zigzag trail and then bolted back in my direction and took a right. She stood on her hind legs and pawed at the miniature stagecoach that was stored in an alcove.

Amy popped out and said, "Good girl!"

"Wow. That was a pretty tough hiding spot and she found you. Then again she did look in the arena for a while."

Amy was patting her dogs head. "That's because I walked around in the arena first, to throw her off."

Kris ran into the barn. "Where are the pool dividers?" she asked.

"In the work shed in a blue container on the back shelf," Amy answered.

Kris said, "Hey" as she ran past me.

"What does she need those for?"

"We have a dock diving competition this weekend. Julie's gonna win all her events."

"Wow. She still flies off the dock?"

"Why not, if she feels like it?"

I shrugged, "Just sayin'…she sure looks good."

* * *

Chapter 24

Three days later I got another email update on Julie:

Julie and I arrived in Columbus Wed afternoon. She swam in the pool and ordered room service. Can you believe the Sheraton didn't have steak?! She had broiled salmon (washed off any oils/seasoning) and steamed green beans. Not as much of a novelty but she enjoyed it nonetheless. She then accompanied my Godson, Joey (he now lives/works in Columbus) and me, to a dinner of our own. She got to view Joey's new apartment and wander in a large, peaceful park with me. It was really a lovely evening.

Julie was disgusted by the comforter that was on our hotel bed... she dragged it off before she could settle in to sleep.

This afternoon she had radiation. She bounced out of the office with a wagging tail, so it certainly doesn't seem like it was too unpleasant an experience for her (she was lightly under during the procedure). She does seem groggier now than usual for this time of day. Her appetite was normal at dinner. I will continue to watch her like a hawk.

Julie's Mom

October 2, 2010:

The next email didn't contain any words, just a photo of Julie dock diving in a competition, wide grin on her face.

October 11, 2010

Julie is still her usual happy, enthusiastic, energetic self. In the last week she participated in her regular Friday night agility class and flyball practice Sunday. She has been swimming, running and playing every day.

We will leave this afternoon for Columbus. Again, I plan on having fun in the hotel pool and providing a luxurious dinner. We may explore the city a little and then Julie will help me do my accounting. Gotta have something to do in a hotel room at night...

Julie's Mom

* * *

Chapter 25

Kris held the horses for me in early November, but Amy and Julie caught up with us a little before I was leaving.

"How are you enjoying your trips to Columbus?" I asked.

"It's hard to be away from the other animals, especially the other dogs. I make sure that Julie has some fun before her treatments." She laughed a little and Kris and I both stared at her.

"Sorry. I was just thinking about something embarrassing I did at the hotel."

We both continued to stare.

"Oh, okay. When I was playing hide and seek with Julie. Well, let's back up. I had just gotten out of the shower when Julie starting taunting me to play. So I put her in a stay and hid. She found me right after several car horns got her attention. I wasn't thinking straight, obviously, because I was still naked and my hiding place was behind the curtain. I had my fat ass pressed against a window." She burst into laughter.

Kris and I exchanged looks and simultaneously burst into laughter.

I coughed. "I appreciate the updates on Julie."

Amy studied me. "Are you being sarcastic?"

"No! I am serious. I feel 'in the loop' so to speak. It's kinda like a diary," I defended.

"I am actually keeping a diary. I don't know why. I keep thinking we'll stumble on something, a treatment, a drug or herb. Something that can cure cancer; and I'll have the sequence of events and stuff all written down."

I didn't say anything. She continued, "I'm not that stupid. I know I am unlikely to find a cure for cancer but she has already made it much farther than any of the oncologists thought possible. Maybe it's the herbal supplement, 'For Life Transfer Factor', I have been giving to her from the day I found out she had cancer. Who knows, maybe I'll write a book."

I smiled. "It'd be better if you told her whole story. You know? Not just the end of the story. That'd be a freaking depressing book."

Amy shrugged. "If you want me to take you off the email list just say the word. No pressure. You won't offend me."

I grinned. "Yes it would."

She nodded. "Yes it would. But it wouldn't change our relationship."

I frowned. "Yes it would."

Again, she nodded. "Okay, it would. But it wouldn't make me think you're an asshole."

"Yes it would."

She chuckled. "It isn't as if it'd make me hate you, wish you were dead, forget we were ever friends and find a new Farrier."

We both started laughing and together recited "Yes it is."

* *

The next update on October 21, 2010 was scary:

> Julie and I arrived at OSU for a "check-up" Thursday morning. As we were trotting up the stairs to the hospital the concierge called out to us, "Good to see you two! How goes the battle?" I smiled and replied, "Great! We are kicking cancer's ass." Two hours later I learned I was wrong.
>
> Julie's cancer has spread aggressively; lymph node, spleen and liver.
>
> Without IV chemo, something I pledged I wouldn't subject her to....she would only be with me for another week to 10 days. I buckled. I could absolutely NOT face losing her in ONE WEEK? We were at the hospital for 10 hours, other than a 1-hour break we took to run back to the hotel for a swim. She had IV chemo, which will hopefully "buy" us another month. Clearly, I am devastated. Often people ask me how Linda (human) & I are such close friends when we are so entirely different....
>
> Well, she heard the news about Julie, dropped everything, and drove to Columbus to be with us, knowing I would be an emotional basket case.

The next email was uplifting:

> Julie and I went to another agility trial. I am trying to squeeze as much fun and life out of our existence right now. She is wearing her contact lenses at agility now, in addition to flyball. Her eyes may be aging some, but you can't tell that she has. Again, two blue ribbons. More important, a happy, playful doggie!!!

After the trial, one of the judges caught up with me. Her dog was just diagnosed with cancer (not the same as Julie's) and she wanted some advice. I told her to get many opinions but admitted Ohio State is one of the best Veterinary Hospitals for canine cancer.

A good deal of my advice was about attitude and making every day, every hour, and every minute count.

She said she didn't know how to get through this, and then asked, "What's your secret?"

I smiled and took a good hard look at Julie.

What an emotional rollercoaster, I thought. The ups and downs could make a person crazy. I would think that the downs were far scarier. After all, we were at the three month mark. The emails continued. There were a few bad days, but many great days. I kept receiving emails, and I appreciated it. Visiting only every six weeks often makes me feel distant from people, and animals I enjoy and care for.

> November 1, 2010:
>
> 11 YEARS AGO TODAY I BROUGHT HOME A BOUNCING BABY YELLOW LAB & NAMED HER AFTER ONE OF MY CLOSEST FRIENDS, JULIE. JULIE WAS AN ABSOLUTELY HORRIBLE, HORRIBLE PUPPY AND SHE CAUSED ME TO "SEEK HELP" (ON SOOOO MANY LEVELS) & MY LIFE WAS CHANGED FOREVER WHEN MY UNDERSTANDING OF DOGS, AND ESPECIALLY JULIE, DEEPENED.
>
> IT WAS ONLY SEVERAL MONTHS LATER THAT JULIE ALERTED ME PRIOR TO A COMPLICATED MIGRAINE HEADACHE. THROUGH HER DEDICATED SERVICE TO ME, AGAIN SHE CHANGED MY LIFE FOR THE BETTER.

DESPITE MANY HARDSHIPS, HAVING JULIE BY MY SIDE THROUGHOUT EVERYTHING (ILLNESSES, FUNERALS, BUYING BATHING SUITS) HAS MADE ME STRONGER.

JULIE ALWAYS SMILES NO MATTER WHAT THE SITUATION. I HAVE BEEN BLESSED!

THIS HAS BEEN A MIRACULOUS AND WONDERFUL 11 YEARS!

After I got this email I went to Pet Smart to get an appropriate Anniversary gift for Julie and Amy. I brought the gift with me on my next visit. I had gotten a toy that can record a voice or anything. I figure Amy would enjoy recording a message to Julie in a toy that could accompany the pooch to chemotherapy. I was already aware that the hospital did not allow Amy to stay with Julie. I knew this was a hardship. Amy didn't do well without Julie.

Amy seemed delighted when Julie tore the wrapping paper off the gift. We played with the toy for a while, recording silly messages. Julie eventually got to her feet, grabbed the toy from my clutches, and took off running with it.

Amy watched Julie run and play. Julie finally settled in the snow and enjoyed her gift, batting with her paws so it would "talk." The love in Amy's eyes when she looked at Julie was deeply moving. I seriously could not imagine what Amy's life would be like when she eventually loses Julie. The two just go together.

Amy broke the silence. "Isn't she the most beautiful dog you have ever known? I'm not saying this because I am her Mother; I seriously think she is just exquisite."

* * *

Chapter 26

The trips to Columbus continued. In early April Julie was as sparkling as ever. Amy yelled hello as she corralled Julie, Linda, and Jill into the SUV to go to agility class. Kris and I both waved.

I looked at Kris. "I hope she never dies."

"Oh she will, and soon."

"How do you know?" I asked

"Well, I have done a little homework of my own. There isn't a dog on record with histiocytic sarcoma that has lived THIS long with that form of cancer." "When Julie dies, so will Amy," She answered.

I raised my eyebrows. "I was talking about Julie."

Kris looked me in the eye and said, "Same difference."

I thought about it and nodded. Then thoughtfully I added, "But Julie is gonna beat this."

* * *

Chapter 27

A my was looming over me when I stood up, exhausted from trimming Hammlet's feet.

I wiped my brow. "I am just finishing up with Hammy. Kris held Lucy and Milton for me but she had to run off to somewhere." I noticed she looked different, but I couldn't put my finger on what it was. A second or two later it hit me. "Is Julie okay?" I asked with alarm.

"Yes, but she isn't feeling well. We had chemo yesterday and this time it made us sick."

I didn't comment on how she combined herself with Julie. I am not sure when she started thinking of herself and Julie as one, but it became second nature to me quite a while ago. It was actually a weird transition. I couldn't pin down the point in time. However, I initially saw them as dog and owner. Then it was dog and mother until I began to combine them in my mind. It was obviously a subtle transition.

"Oh no. I'm sorry to hear Julie isn't feeling well."

Amy shrugged. "She has handled radiation and chemo better than I could have asked. Normally they cannot do chemo more than five sessions, but they felt Julie could handle more as long as they had her on heart medication. Yesterday was eight for us."

I looked at her, not knowing what to say.

"Anyway…" she continued, "I cannot drive without Julie. If I had a heart attack or complicated migraine while driving, I would be hazardous. Plus the cops know my car and I LEGALLY cannot drive without Julie."

"Oh. That sucks." Still not understanding what she wants.

"So could you take a break between horses and drive me to do a few errands?"

I could tell that she was embarrassed to ask so I didn't opt for the opportunity to take any humorous digs at her.

"Sure. I'll just be a few more minutes with Hammy."

I turned my back to her so I could pull Hammlet's left hind leg up and finish trimming his feet.

"I'm going up to the house until you're ready to go," I heard her say softly.

I couldn't help but be a little preoccupied with Julie. I finished Hammlet's feet and replaced him in his stall. I took off my leather apron and holstered my tools in my tool belt before releasing it and tossing it into the back of my truck. I wiped my brow and took a deep breath as I headed up to the house. I rang the doorbell before I read the doormat "Ring bell, win a dog."

I grinned despite my sour mood. I did not mind toting Amy around for an hour or so but I was unhappy that Julie wasn't doing well.

Amy opened the door and four black dogs bounded outside. Coming to a screeching halt before me, they sniffed me thoroughly. One dog jumped up on me and I heard Amy scold, "Debbie! No!" Amy stepped outside and tugged on Debbie's collar to 'encourage' her into a four-footed position. As Amy was gathering the girls I asked, "Where is Julie?"

Almost immediately Julie tore around the corner and ran out to greet me. "She looks great," I offered as I leaned down to receive kisses.

Amy looked up over from gathering the other dogs. "Yeah, she feels fine but she has diarrhea every five minutes."

"Oh. Won't she need to go out to potty when we are gone? I expect we'll be more than five minutes."

Amy rolled her eyes. "Okay, not exactly five minutes. The entire bedroom is covered with crib pads so she will feel free to go to the bathroom there."

"Oh. Okay. Will she go there?" I asked

Amy raised her eyebrows. "She really, REALLY, doesn't want to. She has a great deal of dignity. I may have house broken her too well," she stated as she shut the door behind all the dogs.

We were walking toward my truck. "But service dogs go through very specific training. I thought they were taught to potty on mats in case they were in a position where they could not be outside?"

"Yeah, most are. But I house broke Julie before she truly entered service dog training. She never caught on to that. Again, dignity."

I looked at her and grinned.

"What?" She demanded.

"And yet you have none."

Amy furrowed her brow then thought about it. She smiled.

As we were driving through Geneva I said, "I expect that you will give me directions at some point?"

Amy squinted and looked at street signs as we drove by. "I'm really bad with directions but this shouldn't be too tough. Once we find the street we turn right and it is the only house on that street. Can't miss it."

We drove back and forth for about 45 minutes. Finally, FINALLY, I convinced her to call the woman she wished to meet with and clarify the directions. I heard Amy's side of the conversation and overheard her acknowledge that the house was on Washington in Madison Township, which was 20 minutes away, not Geneva. We drove in silence to Madison. I could see out of the corner of my eye that Amy glanced over at me frequently. She was aware that I was annoyed. When we reached State Route 20, I asked, "Where do we go from here?" "We turn right onto Corner Avenue, then a quick left onto Washington."

When we were on the right road I drove as Amy peered out the window for the right address. "See it?" I asked hopefully.

"Not yet. There are some mailboxes without numbers, though."

"I thought it was the only house on the road?"

"It is. Their mailbox is at the end of their road because THEY ARE THE ONLY HOUSE ON THE ROAD."

I spotted a mailman and, notwithstanding the male stereotypes, I stopped and got directions. When we arrived at the house Amy slid out while I sat in the idle truck. I glared at her as she moved toward the house. I think she could feel my stare because she looked over her shoulder at me and stuck out her tongue.

When she returned to the truck she was carrying a platter of something.

She handed me the large plate as she pulled herself into the truck and said, "There."

I looked down in awe. Cookies! Okay, the trip was worth it.

As Amy reached to pull a cookie out from under the plastic wrap I saw that her face looked pale and drawn. "Are you okay?" I asked.

She nodded as she chewed the cookie. Then she looked over at me, "I'm exhausted. I had to pay the woman who is coordinating Julie's Memorial service. You know; urn, flowers and catering, that kind of stuff. Sherri is SO sweet, but a plate of cookies will hardly cheer me up."

The statement sounded like more than a casual observation. I thought she was referring to the big picture regarding Julie's illness. Julie doesn't look or act sick so it is often easy to forget, until something would jar her back to reality. "Julie looked happy to ME. Why are you planning so far ahead?"

"Not THAT far ahead, and I want to do preparations in advance BEFORE I emotionally crumble. I know something has changed in her. I mean medically. She may not feel it yet, but it has. I watch two of the other girls vie for pack leader. It's natural in a pack to establish new leadership when the current leader becomes too weak, or too sick. I'm in tune to my dogs."

We were both quiet until she added, "You know, everybody seems to have at least an idea of how I love Julie. Nobody has thought about how Julie has loved me. How it is to lose that kind of love, trust. The bond," she seemed to ramble a little. "I have lived with dogs my whole life…"

"People too, though, right?" I quipped.

"No, I was moved to a dog house in the back yard when my brother came along because my parents only had one extra bedroom." With a smile Amy continued, "Dogs, well animals in general, are capable of unconditional love. They don't judge you. I always say that I judge people based on my own personal experiences. You know?" She looked at me.

I nodded. "Yeah, you don't listen to gossip. It's all about how they treat you. I try to do the same, but it is different; I get it."

"You once asked why I swam naked with my dogs and you know what? It caught me off guard because it never occurred to me to wear anything in front of my dogs. I am comfortable with everything, my body image, who I am, my relationship with them. You know, how they are nonjudgmental. It's natural for me to be with them. Actually it's natural to be myself with them. People, not so much. For every 1000 dogs I have met, I have only met two that I didn't trust. You wanna guess the statistics with people?" She looked at me and I shrugged.

"Well, the reality is, despite my cynicism, even research and background checks, referrals and what not, I have only trusted about five people that did NOT let me down. Now dogs, the number was 998 were trustworthy. People 5. Statistics don't lie."

"Maybe you're just a bad judge of character?" I suggested.

She nodded. "There is that, but I also try not to leave much to chance. I was engaged once; before my marriage, I did a credit check. I know that is not romantic, but it saved me a ton of grief because the guy was in debt for more than $250,000. We would have had to register for our wedding at a bank."

"You called it off?" I asked.

"No. I have him tied up in the basement. Of COURSE I called it off!"

"What about employees?" I asked.

She raised her eyebrows. "I have done background checks on everyone before I hire them; doesn't seem to matter, though. There are many creative ways to screw up. Not all of it gets documented. People just don't have good character. I mean, take Julie for instance. When she is clear about what is expected of her she does it. When we track lost dogs, she takes it very hard if she doesn't find the dog. I tried tricking her and tossing an item that smelled like the lost dog somewhere where she could find it."

I looked at her. "Did it work?"

She shook her head sadly. "Nope, she smelled MY scent on it too, so she knew I had had the item. She's not an idiot."

I chuckled. "No. She is definitely NOT an idiot. But she is a dog. People seem to have some kind of twisted chemistry to them. I mean, animals don't kill unless it means their survival. Humans kill for tennis shoes, jealousy, or betrayal. Remember that mother that shot her kid at the end of August because she couldn't find a babysitter for after school was out? Crazy."

"Animals are biological thinking beings. Their thought patterns are more predictable, although I.Q.'s vary," She stated.

I nodded again in agreement. "So you think that animals are perfect beings?"

She thought for a moment. "Perfect natural beings, yes, I guess I do. We should learn from them. So many people study animal behavior…"

I turned and looked at her, "You're one of them."

"...I know, but I work with domestic animals... animals that humans must, or chose to, live with. If people have a better understanding of the psychological as well as physiological parts of any animal they can be understood easily. Not people, though. I majored in Psychology in college."

I raised my eyebrows. "YOU? You studied psychology? What, did you wanna be a shrink or something? I can't see that."

"Or something. Safe; I wanted to feel safe around people so I thought I better study them."

I whistled. "Your parents must've done a number on you."

Shaking her head she said, "No. Well, in some ways perhaps. My brother and I had the ideal childhood. I guess not being exposed to rape and murder and stuff was a good thing, but eventually kids have to face the real world. My brother and I were also raised with very strict moral values. I guess the assumption, as a kid especially, is that is the way everyone works. Not true. The dark side of humans and societies are too much for me. But animals, it is easy to understand them if you pay attention."

"Yeah, but it seems to come natural to you. It isn't so easy for other people," I added.

"I guess they don't see what I see." She chuckled and twisted in her seat toward me. "You know that I was St. Francis of Assisi for Halloween one year? I think it was the fifth grade. Thank God I had friends to protect me from getting my ass beaten."

"He was, or is, the savior of the animals, isn't he?"

She straightened in her seat and nodded. "Yep. Everybody thought I was Jesus, though."

138

I smiled. "Well, same outfit."

She chuckled.

After we drove a little farther her face became haunted again. I urged her to talk about what has been going on. I know she works hard to put on a strong face for Julie. Julie is so sensitive that if she saw her Mother crying all the time it would certainly affect her very negatively. Amy is always with Julie. She even keeps gum handy to mask the adrenaline on her breath so Julie doesn't always know when she is stressed out. She understands a lot about dogs, even more about Julie, obviously. It's the way Julie understands HER that is impressive. Amy seemed to keep her feelings bottled up. I wondered about that. "Do you ever have a chance to let go?"

"What do you mean?" she asked without looking at me.

"To just hide somewhere and cry?" I looked over and saw her frown. "There's nothing wrong with that."

She didn't answer.

I still pushed, "All the trips to Columbus and your regular vet, it must be draining you. I don't know how you do it. Really."

She was still quiet. I broke the silence. "How do you look at that beautiful, happy creature without thinking of the time bomb inside of her? What's your secret?"

Amy turned and produced a faint smile. "I don't do well without her. I literally feel this pull toward her when we are separated."

"That isn't often," I observed.

She nodded, "I know it is psychological, but it FEELS physical, even spiritual." She stared out the window in the direction of home. I am not sure if she was speaking to herself or me when she softly said, "No good without her. I can't face it." She raised her voice for conversation. "It's gonna be harder, harder than any other loss, and I've had A LOT. I just can't face it."

Her head turned as if she was watching something out the window. I assumed she was turning away because she probably had tears in her eyes. She hates that. Then I made another turn and her gaze followed. Another turn, her gaze followed. I knew where we were, but she was terrible, TERRIBLE with directions. Amy seemed to be unaware that she was following the turns on the road. Her stare was vacant. However, it took four more turns for me to realize that the direction of her gaze was steadily adapting toward home, toward Julie.

I felt helpless. "Everything will be okay."

Amy snapped her head toward me and looked me in the eye. "No it won't. I hate it when people say that! Nothing will ever be okay again when she's gone." She swiveled her head back toward the side window and repeated softly, "Nothing."

She wasn't wrong.

"You have had a lot of loss in the last two years. You got through that okay, right?"

Amy again looked at me. Her gaze suggested that I am an idiot. Uncomfortable, I repeated, "Right?"

"Julie got me through." Again facing away from me, just above a whisper, "It was Julie."

We drove the last three miles in silence. As we approached her driveway she said, "In the shower."

"What?" I leaned closer to her.

"I cry in the shower, but I still think Julie knows."

'Of course Julie knows,' I thought, but I kept it to myself.

I watched as a single tear slid down her cheek. She didn't make a move to wipe it away.

Crap.

* * *

Chapter 28

"Hey," I said, as I saw Amy enter the barn. I walked past her as I led Prince to his stall. Julie soon appeared, but looked disappointed when she spotted a horse out of his stall. She started to walk toward the tack room, head held low, before I called her back. Amy didn't comment on the departure from barn etiquette. I was rubbing Julie along her flanks and she was moaning with delight when I looked up at Amy.

Amy smiled at me with her best childlike innocent smile. "Uh oh," I said.

"What?" she feigned innocence.

"You have this look on your face that you need another favor. I am all out of favors. Because of you and your poor navigational skills I was late to two other farms and almost got fired."

Amy looked confused.

I nodded. "Okay. I exaggerated a little. I didn't really get in trouble. I didn't even have anywhere to go after I left here. I just hate driving around aimlessly."

Amy nodded. "That is true. It's annoying when you don't know where you're going. But I know the way to this house. I have been there, like, a hundred times." She sounded reassuring.

She read my facial expression. I was still skeptical.

"Well, never mind then. My truck is in the shop and the car has a flat tire. I wanted to get down here to help you with Lucy and Milton but I may not get back in time. I'll call a cab." She looked at Julie. "I hope she doesn't swallow any chewed gum or something gross in the cab. I would hate for her to get sick on something."

Julie saw her mother move toward the door and headed out of the barn; she ended up leading the way toward the direction of the house.

"I already did Lucy and Milton when Kris was here. No need to hurry back. See ya." I called after her as she trudged through the mud. I felt bad. "Oh, okayyy," I whined to myself. Then I added, as I was closing up the barn doors, "this is why there aren't many nice guys!"

Once again we drove around for a long time, this time in a circle. Finally, Amy pointed. "That's it. I'd recognize the house anywhere."

I rolled my eyes and Julie, sitting between us, thumped her tail. The dog had had her eyes open, taking in all the different scenes, while we drove. It was as if she was trying to memorize her way back. Knowing her Mother, that wasn't foolish.

I pulled into the drive as Amy was riffling through her pockets for a key." Uh oh," she said.

"What?" I asked as I was standing in front of the door of my truck, holding Julie inside.

Amy started to rifle through a bag she had brought along. I was just starting realize that I had not asked enough questions about where we were going and what we were going to do there as she pulled pajamas from her bag.

"Okay," she said looking at me. "Here is the plan. I lost the key to this house last night after I left. I think it got lost in my car when I got the flat tire; and you've seen the inside of my car."

Hesitantly I agreed, "Okayyy. So the key is lost."

"We have to call a locksmith to get us in, so put your performance cap on," she commanded.

My stomach started to churn a little. "By performance cap, you mean…."

"I imagine a locksmith will want I.D. People can't just show up at any house, claim to own it, and have the locksmith let them in."

I shrugged, "You're probably right."

Amy was rubbing her chin thoughtfully. "What I'm gonna say is that my purse is in the house. As long as I walk in the house and around a corner as I am getting their money…" She looked at me. "Do you have any cash on you?"

"Why?" I asked suspiciously.

"Because I cannot exactly pay them with a cheque. I brought $150, but what if it is more? "

I was confused. "So ok, we have to pretend that this is OUR house that we locked ourselves out of, and once we're in you will walk around a corner, and then reappear with cash to pay the guy?"

She nodded her head vigorously.

Still confused. "What if they still want to see I.D.?"

"I'll act totally surprised that it isn't there and start going on and on about where I could have left it."

"Why are you in pajamas and I'm not?"

"We're married. You were outside working on something." She looked around, "Could be anything, like landscape stuff. I was inside lounging around but became mad about something and stormed out here, clutching…" She pulled a ceramic coffee mug from her bag, "my coffee. The door closed behind me and so we are locked out. Okay?"

"So? They won't know the owner's name. It isn't on the mailbox. Use your own identification."

Frustrated she continued to explain. "The mail has their name on it. If I lived here it would be natural for me to stroll to the mailbox to pick up the mail while I am just waiting around outside. I'm gonna put the mail on my dashboard in case he glances at it. Plus, locksmiths might have a crisscross directory to check up on these kinds of things."

I frowned, "How do you know about a crisscross directory?"

She waved me away and casually stated, "I used to be a bounty hunter and it came in handy." I dropped my jaw as she continued on. I watched her mind work as she looked around. "Get all of the stuff from your truck to the car in the driveway."

"Why?" I complained.

"Because your truck plates are from Geauga County, this is Lake County. We can pretend that this is our son's, no, our daughter's car."

"I don't think they'll ask. Why does it have to be a daughter, not a son?"

"Our son is away at college. That is why he left his truck here, duh!" She acted as if *I* were crazy. "EVERYBODY has somebody that has a spare key. If this were our house we would go get our key from a friend or neighbor, or something; unless, our daughter has our key and is on her way and then gets a flat tire. You see?"

I felt a little dizzy. Julie was eyeballing me. I wasn't following this train wreck of thought. "Soooo?"

"Our daughter has our only spare key and she was hurrying over from…" She looked at my truck again. "Geauga County. What is the farthest point in Geauga County?"

I raised my eyebrows. "I dunno. Chagrin Falls?"

"Okay, Chagrin Falls. On her way here she got a flat tire, she's crying, in a bad neighborhood…."

"I must interrupt. There really aren't any bad neighborhoods in Geauga County, but the locksmith may not know that." I was trying to play along.

"Can't risk it, gotta stay close to the truth."

I did a double take. "Close to the truth? In five minutes you have us married with a daughter and son, living in this house with a brand new car, apparently without friends or neighbors that like us because our only daughter lives two counties away and SHE is the one we leave a key with. I haven't even asked where you are going with the flat tire. Oh, I almost forgot; our names are changed too."

She had a blank expression, as if I was being unreasonable.

146

"The flat tire is for two reasons. First, we don't have a daughter, so there has to be a reason she never shows up to help her parents who are, by the way, locked out of their house where they keep their car keys. So we can't drive out to help our daughter change her tire. Don't you see?"

"Sounds like our daughter is a flake. She has been a pain in our ass anyway. She quit college to volunteer at the zoo. She is just as likely to run out of gas as she is to have a flat tire since she never has any money to pay for gas...."

Amy interrupted. "First, she ISN'T a pain in the ass. She is our daughter. She can gain experience at the zoo which will later help her seek employment because she will be better qualified."

I raised my voice. "Better qualified for what? The only thing she will be good at are the tasks at a zoo. How many zoos are there? Huh? The closest other zoo is in Columbus, three hours away and she'll never go that far from us, it took her forever to move out and she was 32!"

Amy started at me. "Well, she isn't a pain in the ass," she stated distinctly. Julie started wagging her tail and looked up at Amy every time she heard the familiar phrase, "pain in the ass."

This made me smile. I had almost forgotten she was with us. She just sat quietly by Amy's side. She was so well behaved that it was easy to relax and even forget that she was here, at a strange location. She could have run off. I think Julie often got taken for granted. She was just always there, an extension of Amy. Or Amy was an extension of the dog. So, we weren't even paying attention to make sure Julie didn't wander off in the strange neighborhood. I felt Amy's eyes on me. I looked at Amy, then away.

I looked at Amy again and she was grinning.

"What?" I asked.

"See... you can do it."

"What?" I was starting to feel like one of the Wart Hogs on the old TV show *'Welcome Back Kotter'.*

Her smile broadened. "You can lie. You really got into it for a while. The gas thing is good. You can call triple A for a flat tire.... But somebody would have to bring you gas. So we'll go with that."

She glanced around. "Where's Julie?" she questioned.

Uh oh, I thought. We should have been watching the dog. Crap.

I was alert now, too. "You go that way, and I'll go this way." Amy shook her head no.

"Why?"

"Because she is in that direction." Amy pointed toward the house. I followed her gaze. Julie was watching us from the back of a sofa that was pushed close to the window. She saw us spot her. She lifted her head and grinned sheepishly. I could see the tip of her tail wagging behind her.

I laughed. Then it hit me. "How did SHE get in?"

Amy shrugged. "I dunno. Let's walk around the house and look around. We'd better get in, or at least get Julie out before she sees one of the cats."

"Couldn't be that big a deal if she does, cats can jump to high places if she chases them."

She stared at me, so I had to ask. "Why? What will happen if she sees a cat?"

"Bad things." She left it at that as we made our way around to the rear of the house.

I spotted it first. "Crap," I complained.

Amy followed my gaze. She halted and sighed. Hands on her hips she looked around. "Well, a doggie door was good enough for Julie but I am not fitting through that."

By now Julie had traced us to the back of the house. She stood in front of a sliding glass door and stared at us inquisitively. We stared back while we considered our situation. Amy retreated a few steps and examined a door handle to another door. She had her face against the glass window in the door when she said, "By GOLLY! I think I've got it!"

"Let's just ask Julie to let us in," I guffawed sarcastically.

"Go ahead and laugh it up. We will." She nodded with confidence.

I had known Amy for eleven years. I actually liked her very much by now. It was a slow process. I also was attached to her horses, and Julie. However, I found myself seriously contemplating tossing all of that away and getting in my truck, and away. I considered Amy. She is nuts! Maybe not dangerous nuts, the way some people think, although I think I could see her killing someone, anyone, in defense of her animals, especially Julie. I contemplated further; then again I probably would too where Julie is concerned.

I continued to watch Amy, a crazy woman trying to lure her dog from outside the house, to a door that led to a kitchen nook inside the house. I glanced over at Julie on the other side of the door. The dog was standing at attention, her eyes on that cat in the distance. Amy knocked on the door off the kitchen. Her dog pulled her eyes off the cat and followed the noise of the knocking. When Julie appeared in front of the kitchen door Amy turned her back and gave Julie a signal for "cha cha." Having taken freestyle classes,

Amy had taught Julie to get in a conga line. She had actually been trying to get all of her dogs to do it in one line, but the end result is that it looks like a bunch of dogs in a group.....well, we'll call it a hug. Julie jumped up, balancing on her hindquarters, paws pressed against the door. Amy turned and faced her dog and put her hand out like a high five, just above the door handle. Julie and Amy exchanged about twenty-two high fives when Julie's paw finally pulled the horizontal door handle down. The dog's weight was enough to push the door open. Amy turned and grinned at me. "Ta da!" She was taking a bow when her lovely dog bolted after the cat but she didn't get far. Fifty feet from us we watched as Julie's hind end collapsed in a sloppy pile. As we were running toward her she looked over her shoulder at us, with her tongue hanging out of the side of her mouth. She was sporting a huge grin. I laughed as I ran toward the dog. Amy beat me to the scene and was helping Julie stand up again. As I bent down to assist I saw Amy's shoulders heave. I thought she was crying until she turned my way. Then I was confused. "Are you laughing or crying?"

"Both," she stated before bringing the attention back to Julie. "Look at her! She isn't even sorry," Amy chuckled.

Julie was walking steadily between her Mother and me. As we rounded the bend toward the front of the house a different cat was waiting at the front door. Julie pushed her shoulders low and forward, her neck straight, and crouched low. She was in take-off position. Amy saw the body language and said "No."

Julie relaxed her hunting stance and looked up at her Mom, still grinning from ear to ear.

"Ya gotta love her," I chortled. And we did.

* * *

Chapter 29

©2010 www.PawPrintsLife.com

Early morning on April 19, 2011, I got a call from Amy. "Milton lost a shoe. Can you get over here and replace it so he doesn't tear up his feet, pretty please?"

"Sure. Don't let him out today, though. I'll be by late because I have a full schedule."

"I thought I'd put one of those safety boots on him. What do you think? It's such a beautiful morning; I hate to leave him in."

"Well, I..."

She cut me off. "I gotta go. Julie fell down the stairs. We're having a rough start to the day." She hung up.

Late that night I pulled down her drive, and was awed by how pretty the property was. There was a full moon and it glistened off the pond water. I could hear frogs chirping. When I got closer to the barn I was startled by the sound of a mournful howl. In the distance I could see the figure of a woman rise from the lawn and walk toward my truck. I parked and slid out of my truck as Amy's tear streaked face became visible in the moonlight. This time there wasn't anybody by her side.

* * *

Postscript

Julie's Memorial Service was held April 23, 2011 at DeJohn & Sons funeral home in Willoughby, Ohio. The ceremony was delayed while the staff hurriedly added more seats as people, even strangers that had simply observed us around town, continued to arrive.

A special *Thank You* to those friends that celebrated with me, grieve with me, and remain my friends, even though the best part of what was left of me, was lost April 19, 2011 at 2:38p.m.

Nothing will ever be the same. I was not wrong.

* * *

Video Title: Celebrating The Life Of Julie

Please use the link below to view the broadcast:

http://www.eventbywire.com/viewevent/?id=555-100

Broadcast Date: 04/26/2011, 3:00 PM Eastern Time

CPSIA information can be obtained
at www.ICGtesting.com
Printed in the USA
LVIW011213220612
287242LV00001B